Tales of the
South Carolina
Low Country

Tales of the

JOHN F. BLAIR, *Publisher*
Winston-Salem, North Carolina

South Carolina Low Country

by NANCY RHYNE

Library of Congress Card Number: 82-9710
Printed in the United States of America

Third Printing, 1989

LIBRARY OF CONGRESS CATALOGING IN PUBLICATION DATA

Rhyne, Nancy, 1926-
    Tales of the South Carolina Low Country.

    1. Tales—South Carolina.   2. Legends—South
    Carolina.
I. Title.   II. Title: Low Country.
GR110.S6R45   1982   398.2'09757   82-9710
ISBN 0-89587-027-4

Contents

Prologue

Virtually everyone is a collector these days, and I am no exception. I once collected record albums and seashells. Later on, my collections became more sophisticated, and I accumulated handmade boxes and silver spoons.

During the 1960s I started collecting stories relating to the coastal area of South Carolina, and I was surprised to find that one of my greatest pleasures came in traveling on remote country lanes and talking with old-timers. They always greeted me warmly, and I was never disappointed in their stories and legends. As well as stories of evil spirits, cures for disease, and tales of rice planters and slaves, many accounts were of killer hurricanes. Today a carnival spirit is in the air when people crowd into hardware stores, super-markets, and gas stations as they get ready for the worst a hurricane can offer. But on October 13, 1893, there were no advance warnings except those that grew out of a local superstition. Some Low Country natives believed that the storm occurred because a mermaid was being held in captivity. Accounts of that storm were recorded by the late Genevieve Willcox Chandler. Mrs. Chandler, a daughter of plantation owners, was educated in Europe. After she had returned to her home in Murrells Inlet, she began recording narratives of people born in slavery and their descendants. Ben Horry, Welcom Beese, Hagar Brown, and many others received her in their homes with pleasure and considered her a good friend, although she was white. As she recorded the stories, she learned to understand Gullah.

Slaves who came to the South Carolina coast brought with them an extraordinary African-English patois. Over the generations, the original dialect was mixed with French variations and gave way to a slaveese called Gullah. There are scholars who believe that Gullah is a corruption of Angola, the name of a country on the western coast of

Africa, formerly part of a Portuguese colony where some of the South Carolina slaves were born. Others believe the word comes from a tribe known as Golas, who lived in Liberia, also on the West African coast.

Along with their dialect, the slaves brought to the South Carolina coast superstitions, customs, and beliefs that helped shape the history and culture of the region. The coastal area became a world rich in spirits such as ghosts, plat-eyes, hants, boo-daddies, and other creatures that roamed the woodlands and cemeteries. For every bend in the inlets that snake their way through the marshes, there was a creature of the night, a cure for disease, or a witchcraft or voodoo practice that was recorded by Genevieve Chandler.

When each of my visits to the Chandler home ended, this gifted storyteller referred me to others who could fill in background information. "See Olive Mancill, a schoolteacher in Georgetown. Her father, old Cap'n Buxton, was captain of Bernard Baruch's yachts." Or, "Slim Thompson, near Pawleys Island, knows all about that." Or, "Mr. Mosier, in a nursing home in Georgetown, was close to the person we're talking about." I went to see these people and also recorded their stories. Their knowledge of the people and places near the coast of South Carolina was quite unlike the stereotype images of the Old South shaped by decades of Hollywood movies and television shows.

In 1975, while doing research at the Library of Congress in Washington, I found in a kind of attic an astonishing collection of tales, superstitions, and practices—the reminiscences of my friend in Murrells Inlet, Genevieve Willcox Chandler, all of which she had meticulously recorded in the 1930s. The files told of life on the South Carolina coast during the 1800s as well as during the early part of this century, and the information added a great deal to the narratives Mrs. Chandler had told me personally.

My collection of folktales is not limited to the stories of Mrs. Chandler. Modern folktales are included. In January, 1980, I went to Beaufort and talked with many of the people involved in the case of the headless corpse. And I spent an afternoon with a witch doctor who explained to me his influence and control over his patients as he deals in potions reputed to have medicinal, poisonous, or magical powers.

Superstitions, customs, and folk expressions survive in the Low Country, and the folklore communicates the flavor and excitement of the early settlers. Low Country folkways may have been American before they were Southern, but because they have endured in the South, and because the dominant legends are linked to plantation heritages, they came to be thought of as characteristically "Southern."

There are still hundreds of people in the South Carolina Low Country who believe in witchcraft and the effects of voodoo practices. Healers who work with dolls, herbs, powder made of ground human bones, and charms have all the sufferers they have the time to treat, and some Charleston pharmacies set aside whole sections for the display of roots, jinx removers, substances used to prevent attack by evil spirits, and other similar items.

In the stories that follow, meet the people in the narratives of Mrs. Chandler and her friends, and the characters in the modern stories as well. Some of the passages are written in Gullah. The patois, as it is spoken today, with its unusual emphasis, pronunciation, and use of idioms, is much the same as it was in the old days. A white person is a "buckra," and food is "bittle." "Um" refers to him, her, and it; "e" means he and also she. The verb steal is "t'ief." To answer the question, "Did someone steal your chicken?'' the answer might be ''E t'ief um.'' To make the excerpts in the following pages more readable, changes have been made in wordage, and spelling has been simplified.

Tales of the South Carolina Low Country

THE DEATH CALL

HEN THE PREACHER ASKED IF ANYONE PRESENT would like to stand up and give his Christian testimony, Uncle Rufus Singleton was always the first one to jump up. Even with his rheumatism, he'd spring up, lean heavily on his stick, and testify.

"I remember when the Lord called me," Uncle Rufus always started his story. "The Lord called me and said, 'Rufus, Rufus, are you ready to go?' And I was ready to go, but the Lord didn't take me then. I am ready to go any time I hear the Lord's call. Any time I hear 'Rufus, Rufus,' I am ready to go."

One night just before a revival meeting service at Gordon Chapel near Murrells Inlet, a group of young people met outside the church. They planned a joke on Uncle Rufus and could hardly get the scheme worked out because they were laughing about it so much. The places by the road on which Uncle Rufus walked home were an important part of the plan—the pine tree, the burial ground with a stone fence around it, the haunted shack, and the cabin in which Uncle Rufus lived with his wife, Aunt Sarah.

As usual, the preacher called for testimonies as the service came to a close. Uncle Rufus was the first member of the congregation to stand up. "Rufus, Rufus," he began, looking heavenward and leaning on his stick. He continued to speak, tears of emotion running down his face, until he had finished his testimony.

As the service ended, Uncle Rufus hobbled to the door of the church, where the preacher was shaking hands with the people leaving the building. The preacher took one of Uncle Rufus's veined hands and held it as he asked the old man about his wife. Rufus made an excuse for her not attending the service. Long ago he had stopped urging her to attend church services, as every attempt to persuade her to accompany him to church had been futile, but he still made excuses for her absence.

Rufus limped out of the building and scuffed across the churchyard. He was walking by a big pine tree when a voice came from behind the tree. "Rufus, Rufus."

Uncle Rufus stopped and put a hand to his ear. He heard the voice again; this time it was stronger and clearer. "Rufus! Rufus! The Father is calling you home."

Uncle Rufus started walking toward home moving along as fast as he could. He was nearly running when he reached the burial ground. A voice came from behind the stone fence. "Rufus, Rufus. Your Father calls you home."

The man didn't give a thought to his rheumatism. Not much farther now, and he would be there. He hurried across the road and ran by the deserted shack, a hut said to be haunted. "Rufus, Rufus," a voice came from within the shack. "Your Father is calling you home."

Uncle Rufus threw his cane into the air and struck out down the road. His eyes searched for the plum bushes that hung over his yard gate.

Aunt Sarah was sitting on the porch when her husband lifted the chain from the post and swung the gate open.

"Why Rufus, where's your cane?"

Uncle Rufus didn't answer. He stumbled as he went in the front door but regained his stride. He was so tired he could hardly move, but he forced himself through the room and back to the bedroom. Going down on a knee, then falling over on his side, he rolled under the bed.

Uncle Rufus held his hands over his ears, but he could not blot out the sound of a voice coming from the window

of his bedroom. "Rufus. Rufus. The Father is calling you home."

Aunt Sarah ran to the bedroom and heard the voice. "Rufus is not here," she shouted. "Who is that? Who wants Rufus?"

"It's the Father. The Father is calling Rufus to come home."

Aunt Sarah put a hand to her mouth. Through trembling fingers she murmured, "I tell you, Rufus is not here."

"The Father is calling Rufus home," the voice said. "But if Rufus is not there, the Father said to send his wife."

Aunt Sarah got down on her knees and grabbed one of her husband's feet. "Rufus, you come out," she scolded, giving the foot a pull. "Come out from under that bed, I tell you. All the times you said you were ready, now come on out!"

The voice continued to call "Rufus, Rufus" as Aunt Sarah gave a harder pull on her husband's foot and Uncle Rufus squirmed back under the bed. Just then Aunt Sarah gave a swift jerk.

"Rufus, you come out from under that bed. You've said all these years you were ready. I never did say I was ready. I'm not ready, and I'm not . . ." A giggle came from outside the window.

"Rufus," Aunt Sarah whispered, "I don't think the Father's calling you. I think it's them young'uns from the church."

Uncle Rufus slid from under the bed and pulled himself up by a bedpost. After a pause and a few deep breaths, he said loudly as he faced the window, "Old woman, you tell the Father I'll meet Him on the porch. Tell Him I've been expecting Him and I'm ready to meet Him."

Aunt Sarah smoothed her apron, then walked behind

Uncle Rufus as they went to the porch. They didn't hear any call for Uncle Rufus to come home, but they did hear the sound of feet scurrying through the yard and down the road.

THE GHOST OF THOMAS YOUNG

THOMAS YOUNG REACHED THE SUMMIT OF THE LOFTiest knoll on Bellefield Plantation and sat quietly on his mount. He was exhilarated and listened to the curious thumping of his heartbeat. Then he said to himself, "Of the eight hundred and seventy acres of this plantation, I perceive this to be the best possible place for me to build a mansion house. Here, on this knoll, with the breathing of the wind, the odors of the forest, and the majesty of Winyah Bay in the distance, the house will sit. It will be most excellent within and without, and my family will treasure living in such a house. I will build it for them."

That was not true and he knew it.

There seemed to be but one necessity in life for Thomas Young: to build a proper house for the visits of any celebrities traveling in the Low Country near Georgetown. Young displayed unusual devotion to people of fame, and he had gone to extents to which no other man would have gone in order to cultivate friendships with men of dignity and importance. As for building a fine house for his family to enjoy, nothing could have been farther from Thomas Young's intention. His wife, although from a wealthy family, was a reserved and quiet girl who shunned society, and his daughter was a child.

Several times each day Young rode to the bluff on the plantation and looked with satisfaction at the site overlooking Winyah Bay. Those who knew him said nothing else compared with his passion for the spot of land where he planned to build his mansion.

One day Young got off his horse and walked about the

knoll examining it in detail, as he had done on many previous occasions. It was a dark and somber place among the mournful trees. In broad daylight the sun only dappled the rich, moist soil of the forest floor.

Suddenly, Young noticed the skeleton of a house in the woods. It was obvious that construction of the house had not been completed, but the framework seemed exceptional in some ways. There were two chimneys, tall and square and of hard brick, and the position of the building was seen as an advantage. The southeastern angle extended forward so that when looking from inside the drawing room or dining room, whichever was to occupy the position, the eye would at once take in Winyah Bay.

At first Young was puzzled and angry. He wondered who, before him, had chosen this knoll for a home, and he was curious as to why he had never glimpsed the framework before. Had trees and undergrowth obscured the skeleton house so that he had not seen it in the dim light that seeped through the trees? It was an alarming discovery, and Young had to suppress the belief that the beginnings of a house had loomed up out of nowhere.

But Young could not deny that he was deeply attracted to the skeleton house. He experienced such intense emotion that, he concluded, it would be unthinkable to destroy the building; he must add to it. But, he also concluded, he must put first things first.

Young surmised that he could afford to build the mansion of his dreams only after he became a rich man. In order to increase his income, he would have to cultivate the rice fields on the rivers adjoining his plantation.

Clearing the swamps for rice fields was a nearly impossible task. Slaves had to cut and remove from the fields every bit of the tangled vines and trees that had grown there for centuries. Then the fields would be harrowed and prepared for a springtime planting of tender rice seed. From

the time of the planting, it would be several months before the harvest and sale of the rice in Charleston.

Since the nearest market for rice was in Charleston, and the rivers around Georgetown did not connect with the other rivers around Charleston to provide an inland route, the product had to be transported via the ocean, which was called the "outside route." The idea came to Young that if he and some other planters could go into a partnership and buy a schooner, they would have available the means with which to get their product to the market easily and quickly. While he was negotiating for a partnership in a schooner, his slaves were clearing the swamps and forming the fields. Busy though he was, each day Young visited the knoll on which his mansion would stand. So familiar did the dream house become that he seemed intimate with every corner and part of it.

The mansion would be in the same architecture as Charleston's finest residence—the Miles Brewton house on King Street. But it would be more exquisite than the Brewton house. The drawing room would be on the second floor to catch the breeze, and a Waterford crystal chandelier would hang from a ceiling decorated in carved medallions of much detail. The ornamentation of the woodwork would be fine and delicate. This room would be entered from a piazza, or porch, where double flights of wide steps would extend from the porch to a stone platform at the ground. And surely there must be a piazza facing south, facing Winyah Bay, to match the one on the north where visitors would be welcomed.

As he thought about it, visitors traveling the curving roadway through the trees would not be aware of the mansion on the hill until their carriages came around the curve and stopped at the courtyard to be built where Young now stood, and at that very moment they would see the mansion looming high above them.

Perhaps some members of the royal family in England would visit Bellefield house. And if the word now spreading was true, if in actuality President Washington was planning to tour the South Carolina coastal area in a year or two, he might dine here.

In his daydream, Young envisioned Washington's coach stopping at the courtyard. Servants attended the horses, and the coachmen and outriders, and Young escorted the president up the steps. Young's wife and daughter waited on the piazza to greet the famous visitor. After the introductions, they would step over the threshold and go into the dining room, where every food considered a delight to the palate would be waiting to be served along with wines and ales. Oh! To make Washington's acquaintance and enjoy his confidence would be intensely exciting.

When Young emerged from his reverie, he had taken leave of his composure. He made plans for erecting the mansion right then. If he didn't get his mansion completed by the time of Washington's visit, the president would surely be entertained at Clifton, the home of King Billy Alston. Up to now Clifton was the most magnificent of all the Low Country houses, and that plantation would be a likely place for a president to be entertained. Young winced at the thought.

Young called his slaves from the rice fields. Trees were cut and squared into beams. The sound of the broadax reverberated in the forest. Young supervised the removal of every tree from the site where the house was to stand. He was often pale and frequently passed a hand over his brow as though he couldn't continue the supervision and work much longer. But he worked on the mansion each day, and when the day ended, he continued to work into the night.

As the work progressed, and after the flooring had been put in, the slaves were not allowed to leave the construc-

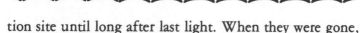

tion site until long after last light. When they were gone, Young would take a lantern from a rafter and walk about the rooms, inspecting each stud and beam that had been hoisted into place that day. He didn't go to the modest home he occupied with his wife and daughter until he had examined every detail of the day's work.

One day as Young left the construction site, he was desperately drowsy and had a wretched headache. He made his way through the forest to his home, where he ate a light supper and went immediately to bed. As he began to relax, his eyes rolled back in his head with the lids and brows making no move. A sweat covered his body. Sometime during the day that followed, Thomas Young was found dead in his bed. His death was attributed to overwork.

Labor on the mansion stopped. For a time everything was in a state of chaos. There was some confusion as to the advantage of resuming the work on the rice fields and as to the way in which the business portion of the plantation should be operated. Bellefield Plantation remained in this state until it was purchased by King Billy Alston of Clifton Plantation.

From the many boats traveling the Waccamaw River, Clifton house could be seen on a bluff. Nearly everyone took notice of the double piazzas with their roofs supported by white columns. It was difficult to conceive how all this beauty had been attained. Visitors, who nearly always arrived by boat, were escorted up the hills of thick, velvety green lawns to the terraces that had been landscaped with laurels, magnolias, and oaks. From the terraces they went up the steps to the piazza of the magnificent mansion, where they paused to look back at the emerald grass sloping down to the Waccamaw. With such a mansion as Clifton, it was inconceivable that King Billy would give a thought to completing the house at Bellefield.

One day a rider arrived at the Clifton piazza. He was weary and in need of nourishment. The rider was invited to come into the mansion and have a glass of sherry. After he had regained his strength, he handed a note to King Billy. The note said President Washington was touring the coastal area and would dine at Clifton on April twenty-ninth.

Washington arrived at Clifton. Just after he had stepped from his coach, servants took the reins and led the horses in the direction of the barn. King Billy escorted Washington up the steps. The president spoke to Mrs. Alston, then turned to gaze down at the lawns and thousands of acres of rice fields, which were in view although they were some distance away. For a few minutes King Billy and Washington discussed the planting of rice. Then Washington stepped over the threshold and they all went into the dining room.

The table was set in blue-and-white porcelain dinnerware and crystal that sparkled in the sunlight streaming through the ceiling-to-floor windows. Servants, wearing their usual clothing of green plush faced with red and edged in gold trim, served ham from a silver tray, oysters from a deep dish, and other foods that were the best the Low Country had to offer. King Billy was fond of social life and devoted to politics, and the meal stretched into the afternoon as the men talked at length about many subjects. It was late in the day when the president was escorted by his host to the Waccamaw River, where Washington continued his journey, now by boat. King Billy returned to his mansion and reflected on the wonderful visit with the president. Long after nightfall, about the time that King Billy was preparing for bed, a man who was walking through the woods at Bellefield Plantation saw the figure of a man, carrying a lantern and inspecting the framework of the Bellefield house. Although shockingly pale, the phantom nevertheless displayed a fierce and scowling expression.

There were rumors of other eerie things happening at the site of the Bellefield construction. A plat-eye was said to be a frequent visitor. Few of the people who lived in the cabins on the plantation denied the existence of ghosts, particularly a creature they called a plat-eye. As one of them explained:

There's ghosts and there's plat-eye. Mattie saw a plat-eye. First he was a white cat and the next thing she knew he was a big old white dog with red eyes. It was a plat-eye all right. Terrible.

A runaway slave told of seeing Young, carrying a lantern and inspecting the unfinished house during the night. He was so frightened that he returned to his master and begged forgiveness for running away.

There were many stories told about the unfinished house, one of them concerning a white owl that made its home in the structure. It was from this story that Thomas Young's dream house got its name—the White Owl House.

Just after dark one gusty evening, Young was seen at the White Owl House examining the bricks of one of the chimneys. He carried a lantern, and after he had scrutinized the bricks in the chimney, he explored the premises. A month later, Young was again seen at the White Owl House. He took the lantern from a rafter and held it as he stood at the place where the porch would have been, had it been built. Suddenly, another figure materialized. With a sweep of an arm, Young escorted the wispy figure over the threshold and into the house. Two sets of footsteps were heard. Gigantic footfalls seemed to follow other, lighter footfalls, and the heavy crunch-crunch did not synchronize with the progress of the other phantom's feet and could not have been an echo.

During the following years there was scarcely a month

that someone's eyes didn't fall upon the countenance of Thomas Young in the recesses of the White Owl House, always carrying a lantern, inspecting the work of the mansion or escorting a visitor through the house. Finally the ghost was regarded with respect and his presence was accepted because of his obvious grief and his unhappiness that his unfinished house would never be a scene for the entertainment of celebrities.

Bernard Baruch, a man who had made millions on Wall Street, bought Bellefield in 1905 at a time when he was putting together the jigsaw of plantations known as Hobcaw Barony. His eldest daughter, Belle, took an interest in Hobcaw Barony, and her father conveyed Bellefield Plantation to her.

Belle Baruch learned to fly, bought a plane, and obtained her pilot's license. She flew over the plantation until she learned where the herds of deer could often be seen. "Look at the deer!" she would scream to a companion as they flew overhead. She also became an accomplished yachtsman, winning many trophies in that sport. But Belle Baruch's passion was horses.

She rode horses, trained horses, and showed them all over the world. In 1930 and 1931 she received the President's Cup and Republic's Cup as winner of the classic competition in the Paris horse show. She won more than three hundred prizes in France and other countries.

In 1936 Belle began to search for the perfect place to have a house constructed for herself. The location must also lend itself to a fine stable in close proximity to the house. She searched the landscape from her airplane, which she piloted just over the treetops, and she rode her famous horses over the plantation grounds. One day as she was riding, she saw what appeared to be a path, and yet, she wondered if it could be considered a path at all. She leaned forward, her head just under the tree limbs, and urged her horse onto the path through thick foliage. Pressing on, trying to remain within the confines of the road, if indeed it was a road, her head dodging undergrowth, she came to the peak of a knoll.

There, in the foliage, was the framework of a house that had obviously been constructed many years before. Amid the symmetrical oaks, it was a neat and graceful place with a fairylike avenue extending to Winyah Bay. What to make of all this, of course, she did not know.

As she observed, piece by piece, the structure on the summit with two tall, slender chimneys and a glimpse of water and of sky, she fancied a new house in the setting. Lifting the reins, she turned her horse and started back to her father's house. She couldn't wait to tell him of her discovery.

Baruch helped his daughter get the plans for the building of her house underway. As Belle got more involved in the planning, people began to tell her the stories of the White Owl House. The ghost of Thomas Young visits the house, they told her, and he thinks he is finishing the house he started a hundred and fifty years ago. His greatest desire is to entertain celebrities in the house. Belle thought about it and decided that the ghost stories would add even more charm to her new house.

When the blueprints were completed, architects told Belle emphatically that the skeleton of the White Owl House must be dismantled. The only place for a new house was in the exact spot where the skeleton now stood, and there was no way the framework of Young's house could be properly incorporated into the new structure. If she wanted to have the advantage of the elevation and the view, then the old house would have to go. The White Owl House was pulled down.

The new house fitted perfectly into the setting. The

library had lofty beams on which mounted native animals were placed. Deer antlers were attached to the high beams. A stuffed bobcat crouched on the hearth. And the walls were adorned with paintings of Belle's favorite horse, Souriant.

The whole house, including the wings, was built of brick and wood. The shades of aged brick and stained wood blended into the colors of the natural setting. Not ten steps from any of the main doors stood giant oaks draped in Spanish moss. Jasmine vines of unequaled luxuriance grew from one tree to another.

On Easter Sunday in 1944, when World War II was flaming in Europe, a car pulled up to the Bellefield entrance. A passenger in a black cape got out and was carried up the steps and placed in a rolling chair. Belle Baruch stood on the piazza and greeted her famous visitor—President Franklin D. Roosevelt.

Roosevelt had chosen a time of great peril to visit this place. Plans were being made for the June 6, 1944, invasion at Normandy. Under the stress of the impending invasion, the president was losing weight. He had a nagging cough, and was bone-tired. It was for reasons of health that he accepted Bernard Baruch's invitation to visit him at Hobcaw Barony, and it was while he was there that he asked to visit Belle at Bellefield.

Roosevelt's chair was rolled to the fireplace in the Bellefield library. He had suffered polio as a young man and was crippled by the disease. He moved about in a rolling chair.

As it was a cool day, a fire crackled in the fireplace. The stuffed bobcat sat at Roosevelt's feet. Belle and her visitor entered into a long, earnest, and uninterrupted conversation. She listened to stories of his earlier life at Hyde Park, at Albany, and still later in Washington. He gave his con-

centrated attention to her narratives concerning her yachting experiences, as yachting was a sport he had once enjoyed.

The sun had gone beyond the oaks and a chill was in the air when a servant brought into the room a tray with a pot of tea and several slices of cake with icing made of berries that had grown wild on the plantation. Enjoying cake and tea, Belle and Roosevelt talked on and on.

It was quite late in the evening when Roosevelt summoned his driver and asked to be taken back to Baruch's house. With a wave of her hand, Belle dismissed for the day a servant at the same time that Roosevelt was rolled from the library to the foyer and onto the piazza. From the piazza, the president was carried, rolling chair and all, to the limousine at the foot of the steps. After he was seated next to the driver, the rolling chair was put into the trunk of the car.

The car rolled through the trees. Belle stood on the piazza, waving good-bye to her guest. Unknown to her, the servant whom she had dismissed only minutes before stood in the shadows watching.

Belle closed the door, but the outside lights remained on. The servant's hair stood on end as she realized that a form coming from the house was no human body. He carried a lantern, and the servant could see the pallor of his eyebrows and hair, and his long jaw. The mouth was large, and there was a kind of chuckle as the ghost walked by.

Thomas Young had made his final visit to the mansion on the knoll. Perhaps he had at last realized his dream. For until her death in 1964, Belle Baruch entertained world-famous people in the very location and manner that had been Thomas Young's greatest desire.

A MOST DANGEROUS PRANK

I T'S A STORY THEY TELL IN CHARLESTON, WHERE, AS THE natives say, the Ashley and Cooper rivers meet to form the Atlantic Ocean, and where great plantations still exist on the mighty rivers.

During the afternoon of September 10, 1974, two brothers who lived in Charleston visited Runnymede Plantation on the south side of the Ashley River near the world-famous Magnolia Gardens. The plantation visit was a kind of end-of-summer outing, as the brothers were leaving the following morning to attend school in another state.

The students walked along the banks of the river, occasionally looking back at the Runnymede manor house surrounded by live oaks, broad planted fields, and a proliferation of foliage. They seemed to be mentally occupied with, and perhaps discussing, the heritage of the plantation that had been carved from a wilderness in 1705 by the Cattells. From the Cattell family, the plantation passed to the ownership of Abraham Ladson and then to Lambert Lance. From Lance the property was purchased by John Julius Pringle, the distinguished Charleston lawyer, who was Speaker of the Assembly in 1787. Pringle found it necessary to build a new manor house when the former one burned. When his fine house was completed, Pringle spoke of naming it Susan's Villa, in honor of his wife, but the final decision for a name was Runnymede.

In later years this plantation was the home of Major-General Charles Cotesworth Pinckney, who had been born in Charleston in 1746 and began his schooling in England in 1753. Pinkney studied law at the Temple in London and

was admitted to the bar. When he returned to South Carolina, he was elected a member of the Assembly and later became a member of the Provincial Congress.

Runnymede, looming magnificently on the landscape in front of the students, was equally as impressive as the noted families who had lived there.

One of the chief amusements of the students was sauntering along the marshlands and in the forests in quest of Low Country wildlife, such as alligators and ducks. Their visit to Runnymede resulted in an excursion of this sort, and as they walked deep into the forest they came upon a Negro burial ground. On the mounds of earth above the remains of the people who had been buried in the remote graveyard, there had been placed certain personal items which had belonged to the deceased people. Although the graves were those of people who had been buried in recent years, the custom of placing personal items on graves is rooted deep in Africa. It is not uncommon to see plates, cups and saucers, and drinking glasses on a mound of earth over the remains of a woman. And tools are sometimes placed over the remains of a man. Other items that are sometimes placed on graves include the favorite chair of the deceased person, or a bottle of medicine and the spoon with which the remedy passed to the mouth of the person who was buried in the grave. A Low Country man explained the custom: "This is for to keep them from comin' back for these things."

For some unexplained reason, a rather nonchalant mood overtook the students. Perhaps they were so looking forward to an airplane ride to Charlotte the following morning that they abandoned their sense of propriety. But whatever it was that motivated their frolicsome mood, they chose to play a most dangerous prank. They could not have helped knowing that it is believed implicitly by hundreds of people living in the South Carolina Low Country that if

18

one of the personal items is removed from a grave, or if a cemetery item is tampered with in any way, retribution by the spirit of the dead person will be not only swift, but quite dreadful. Yet, the students removed a drinking glass from a burial mound and took it back to their home in Charleston.

When the parents of the students saw the object, they immediately questioned the young men, who confessed to the prank. The parents were alarmed. They well knew the strong influence certain superstitions and black magic had on some of the people living at Runnymede Plantation. Many of them had had little contact with the world away from the plantation, and they held on to superstitions, customs, and beliefs that had been handed down to them from their ancestors.

A call was placed to the plantation. The owners of Runnymede insisted that the item be brought at once to the burial ground and placed in its original position. This was done. But word was spreading by the plantation grapevine that an object had been taken from a grave in the forest. Vengeance by the spirit of the dead person was probably already at work.

The following morning at 6:30 the students boarded Eastern Airlines Flight 212 for Charlotte. The plane ascended higher and higher, and when Charleston was far below, stewardess Colette Watson walked down the aisle serving coffee to the passengers. The boys sipped the coffee and looked from a window, but because of heavy fog there was almost no visibility.

It seemed only minutes before the pilot's voice came over the public address system saying, "Please fasten your seat belts. We'll be descending in the glide path for Douglas Municipal Airport at Charlotte in a few minutes." But up in the cockpit, the pilot and copilot were discussing politics, and used cars, and almost any-

thing else that had nothing to do with landing the plane.

Just then a passenger saw a part of a pine tree fly by his window. A few moments later the plane crashed in a field of corn three miles south of Douglas Municipal Airport.

A woman who had been thrown clear of the wreckage called for someone to come and pray the Lord's Prayer with her. A man who had also been thrown clear of the plane called for help.

Ten minutes later some of the people near Gate 5 began checking at the ticket counter. Where were the passengers? Had Flight 212 arrived? The scream of a siren was heard in the distance.

In the field south of the airport a blanket of fog hung over the aircraft. Suddenly, there was an explosion. The plane became a ball of fire. Inside, seventy-two people were dying, including the two students from Charleston.

Word of the accident reached Runnymede Plantation quickly. The crash of Eastern Airlines Flight 212 was no surprise to the people who buried their dead in the burial ground in the forest. The crash was, they explained, a reasonable and not unexpected reprisal by the spirit of the dead person whose grave had been violated the day before.

THE MERMAID STORM

(As If Told by Dr. J. Ward Flagg)

There is a legend about the mermaids that swim in the ocean at Murrells Inlet, South Carolina. From the moment a sea maiden is taken from her native environment, a storm builds in the West Indies. Vicious, gaining momentum, the gale follows a path to Murrells Inlet, a village under moss-draped oaks. If the mermaid is not released from captivity by the time the storm reaches the Inlet, winds unleash their energy and great rods of lightning seem braced by struts of fire. The rains come faster and faster, and the water level rises until the mermaid is washed back to her home in the Atlantic. An unearthly pink glow ridicules the destruction spread on the land. Then the sun comes out.

I NEVER TELL MY STORIES NOW. I AM OLD, AND IT IS permissible for me to sit and think of that day, Friday the thirteenth of October, eighteen hundred and ninety-three. Who else is there who remembers that day? But I remember it well.

After I graduated from the Medical College of South Carolina in 1881, I came home to Brookgreen Plantation. I was the fifth of the Flagg family who graduated from the medical college in Charleston. Father hung the document conferring my degree, with my name, Ward Flagg, lettered in gold, next to his in the library. Father, too, was a physician. He was a descendant of Dr.

Henry Collins Flagg, who entertained George Washington at Brookgreen. Father, as well as Mother, was a part of the Brookgreen connection.

We lived on a part of the plantation called "the farm." Mother had inherited "the farm" and the seashore portion of the plantation, Magnolia Island, after her father's death. Grandfather Joshua John Ward was the greatest rice planter in the South Carolina Low Country. He was a millionaire when most people didn't know how to spell the word. He perfected the big-grain rice that made millionaires of other Waccamaw River rice planters.

The three of us were getting ready to go to Magnolia Island for the month of October. No, as I think back, there were four of us. Clarissa Horry, Mother's waiting girl, was asked to join us. But only because of her loyalty to Mother did she agree to go. She told Mother she had heard some talk that a storm was on the way to Magnolia Island. The people who lived in the row of cabins called the quarters believed Father had captured a mermaid and was holding her captive in a shed back of our cottage on the beach. Mother couldn't seem to disguise the annoyance that crept over her when Clarissa said, "The rain's a-comin' now, and a cyclone'll follow." No amount of reasoning on Mother's part could persuade Clarissa of the absurdity of the notion. It strikes me now that some of the people in the quarters still believe storms come as a result of mermaids being held captive. When Clarissa went so far as to describe the mermaid from accounts of eyewitnesses, Mother's annoyance gave way to sadness, and, after reflection, gentleness.

Just before we left the plantation for the seashore, Mother invited three of her nieces, the Weston girls, to go along. Their mother was Alice Ward Weston, Mother's sister. As the girls were studying piano, Mother promised to have the Chickering moved to the beach so that they could continue their daily practice. The girls agreed to join us for the month of October at the seashore.

I often dream I am back on that day we went to Magnolia. I can still feel the fear crawl over me. Father and Mother didn't speak for a full fifteen minutes as they went about the rooms choosing what they would take to Magnolia Island to amuse themselves. I cannot remember a time when they did not follow the same procedure and select the very same things to take to the seashore. Father scrutinized each of the medical journals in a stack on his desk as he picked out the ones he would take with him. I knew he would take all of them. He had an excellent variety of journals, and I was aware that he would be unable to leave a single one of them at the plantation. I didn't doubt what he would do next. He went straight to the All Saints Church vestry book, took it from the shelf, and placed it on top of the complete stack of medical journals. While staying at the cottage on Magnolia, he always worked on entries of births, deaths, and marriages in the parish at the same time Mother worked on the Flagg Family Bible.

Just then Mother came into the room with the Bible and a box of notes. From the notes, she would record in the Bible records of the people living on the plantation. Because she had her hands full, I offered to carry her tatting box to the carriage. In her later years she made yards and yards of tatting lace, which she sewed on linens. I look around the room now and see linen table scarfs edged in Mother's tatting.

During the first week of our stay on Magnolia, Clarissa consistently complained about the rain. More than once she mumbled, to no one in particular, "It's a-comin'," referring to her cyclone. Mother, in a moment of indulgence, offered to accompany Clarissa to the shed to see for herself that there was no mermaid there. Father didn't know about Clarissa's prediction that a storm would descend on the land and free a mermaid being held captive. We didn't tell him, as he would have been less than tolerant of such a superstition.

We had been on Magnolia more than a week when one day there was a sudden change in the weather. Rain became a downpour, and the gradually rising wind gusted in on a high tide. The day that had been uncomfortably warm grew chill.

That night at supper the roar of the wind and the gravity of comments threw me into desolation. Usually, I enjoyed the casualness and intimacy of the family at meals while at the seashore. But that night, as the flame of the lamp jumped and flickered in gusts of wind that blew in through crevices around the windows, Mother talked about the last of the rice crop. She said if rice stalks had been cut and left lying on the stubble in the fields, the crop would be ruined; but that the field workers probably had stacked the stalks of rice on racks in the barnyard. Father talked about All Saints Episcopal Church and some of the tragic incidents of its history. But the vestry minute book had always been kept intact, he said, and if it were ever destroyed, it would be a terrible loss to the parish. Then he reminded us that sometime while we were at Magnolia we should take a look at the book on the table in the hallway. Having nothing to add to the conversations, I kept quiet.

Soon after the meal, Mother had a word with her nieces about their practice of the piano, and then she suggested they go upstairs to bed. She also dismissed Clarissa. After they were gone and Mother, Father, and I were in the sitting room, the lamp flickered from a draft of air. Rain hit the window panes like bullets. There was just a moment when Mother seemed uncertain. She looked at Father sharply but did not speak. The sound of the surf blending with the roar of the wind was desolate. After a moment

Mother's thoughts appeared to flash suddenly into the cottage of my brother and his family south of our house. "I have no way of knowing," she said, "but I believe Arthur, Jr., will be making any necessary preparations for an October gale." Her eyes then lost some of their usual lustre. "There are so many in Arthur's house tonight, considering the children and the guests." Father looked over his spectacles and almost said something but didn't. It wasn't long before the three of us went upstairs and retired for the night.

It might have been midnight, or perhaps later, for I had taken no note of time, when a sob—low, gentle, but very distinct—startled me from my slumber. I felt that it had come from the hallway outside my room. I strained my hearing, but there was no repetition of the sound. A minute or two elapsed, and then I heard voices. "This is unendurable," someone said, obviously speaking of the sounds of the wind. Then I heard Mother's voice coming from her room. "If this night is bad for you, use your faith in God to occupy your thoughts." They all went back to their rooms, but I don't think sleep came. I must have been a rigid figure on the bed as I lay there and listened to the thunder, which I thought surely meant there was an earthquake at sea.

The night waned; and still, with a bosom full of agonizing thoughts, I remained gazing into the darkness.

Before first light, I stood at my bedroom window, thinking of the storm barely six weeks earlier when dozens of people in this very parish had lost their lives. The dawn came almost unnoticed to a day that had no real beginning. Chunks of sea foam blew to a fare-thee-well in all directions. Turbulent swells came closer and closer to the house. The sea was a mass of liquid disturbance. Others left their rooms and went downstairs, but I remained at the window. The scene was altogether beyond description.

I couldn't direct my eyes to anything other than the wild water rushing toward the house.

Clarissa was serving hominy when I finally went into the dining room. Mother did not turn her radiant smile on me as she usually did in the mornings. I tried not to show my concern for our safety. I think we were all feeling a sense of imminent danger, but not one of us, especially not Mother, Father, or I, could set aside our pride, or whatever it was, to speak of evacuation. Had we been meek, we would have abandoned the cottage and fled to the safety of the plantation hours ago. But we could never have done that. Fortunately, we had no idea of the tragedy the day would bring.

Just then a great vibration shocked us to attention. Clarissa looked at me and responded in a high-pitched voice. "Oh, Doc Wardie, that gale's gwine kill every head in this house. Gwine wash 'em to sea!"

"Get upstairs," Father shouted. "Everyone, upstairs!"

"The boat," Mother cried. "Get the boat."

"Too late," Father answered, urging her to leave the room with a gesture of his hands.

We had just gathered in a bedroom at the top of the stairway when the house again quivered and bricks from the bedroom fireplace tumbled into the room. "To the roof," Father screamed. But just then I caught sight of the cedar tree, which I had planted as a child. "No," I countered. "Into the tree by the window. It's still rooted." Although the tree was lurching in the wind, I figured if we could get to it, and hold on while working our bodies along the limbs, we would stand a chance of survival. There was no time to waste.

I pushed the window up and placed a board between the window frame and the window sill to hold it up. My hands were already damp and cold. For just an instant I closed my eyes. My heart was beating desperately. The intensity of the wind stifled me, and I breathed deeply. I wondered if I could physically manage to get into the tree and help the others to whatever safety it offered. I had always taken good care of myself, determined to remain as healthy as I could. Then there rushed upon me a thought that filled me with terror. I forced myself to open my eyes, and my worst thought was not confirmed. The tree was still there. It was still rooted. Deliberately, I ordered myself to go for the tree.

While holding on to the window ledge, I backed out of the window. When my feet touched the rim of a shutter hanging by a downstairs window, I realized the shutter offered a kind of foundation from which I could reach for the cedar. I moved my feet about until they were securely supported by the shutter. Then, in a flash, I turned and grabbed the tree. I quickly encircled a limb with an arm and extended my other arm toward the upstairs window as I shouted instructions to Father. Leaning from the window, he held onto first one and then another of the Weston girls until they had passed from the window to the shutter. With my free arm I pulled them into the tree. Clarissa followed the girls. As for Mother, there was a moment in her state of anxiety when she seemed to alter her will to leave the window. She was pale and trembling. Then, as though she were animated by some spiritual force, a wry smile touched her lips, she turned her back to the window, and Father helped her out. The wind whipped her skirts around her ankles. She held firmly to the window ledge and extended a foot toward the shutter. But she withdrew the foot as if unsure as to which foot to advance first. "Now!" I shouted, reaching for her. She lowered both feet to the shutter, and as she turned toward the tree, I grabbed her and pulled her into it. Father was the last one to leave the window and come into the tree.

All our clothes were torn and pulled from our bodies by

the waves thrashing about us. Suddenly my cousin Elizabeth paled; her small body shivered violently. "I feel so ill," she cried. I reached for her with my left hand, calling, "Live for your mother's sake," but it was too late. She had slipped from the tree into the mass of churning water.

After what seemed an eternity but was probably only moments, the cold drained my energy and I felt relaxed and in need of sleep. I admonished myself to keep all my senses alert and kindle in the others a determination to survive.

A wall of water came rushing toward us, and when Father saw it, he said, "It's forty feet high." Mother turned to see the wave and lost her grasp on the tree. Seeing her predicament, Father let go of the tree and held his arms to her. As the wave crashed, Mother was swept into his arms. In their last embrace they were sucked into the whirlpool that surrounded us. I was numb, half-conscious by then. I don't remember much of what happened after my parents were swept away. But I do know that when the tide finally turned and the sun broke out from behind the clouds, only Anne Weston, Clarissa Horry, and I were still holding onto the beach cedar.

I was told that when help came to us, I was unable to slacken my hold on the tree limb and my fingers had to be pried loose one-by-one. All the cottages on Magnolia Island, except for one on a high dune back from the sea, were destroyed. My brother and his wife and five of their six children all lost their lives. My brother's wife's body was found entombed in a roll of wire.

Those who could put aside the horror of the past hours and walk along the sandy shore found treasures. Among other things, a colorful Indian axe had washed ashore. And the All Saints vestry minute book, soaked with salt water and torn, was half buried in sand.

For all the people who came to my house in all of these

years and asked to hear the narrative of the Mermaid Storm, the story ended at this point. But, for you, I will finish this story of the past. I am living it again so vividly, it seems as though it happened only yesterday.

Clarissa continued to tell her colorful story of the mermaid being held captive in the shed. I had lost the family I had loved more than anyone. They were gone. I would sometimes close my eyes and see the three of us: Mother writing in the Bible, Father reading medical journals, myself in the background.

One day Tom Duncan, an old family retainer, came to me at "the farm" and said he would take care of me. He had lost his mother, Mom Adeline, and a brother, Ripper, in the gale. I told him I was perfectly capable of taking care of myself, but he told me it would be good to have someone about, someone whom I could trust. So it was settled.

Tom cooked my meals and cleaned the rooms. Day-in and day-out I watched him, talked with him; so great was my grief that I was unable to leave my house. For me there was no joy. I could only feel sadness over the loss of my loved ones. One day, after I had remained inside for more than two years, a message came for me. Most of the children on the plantation were afflicted with worm infestation, and treatment was needed. I thought of leaving the house and I felt fear, but the plight of the children had to be reckoned with. I sank to my knees and remained there until some inner force bid me rise. I felt the blood rush to my cheeks as I stood up and took measure of myself and my departed family. Through no fault of mine they had lost their lives. But life had already given them a great deal. I took my medical bag and left the house. It was a triumph.

NOTE: Dr. J. Ward Flagg died in 1938. Many prominent people in South Carolina, including the governor, attend-

ed his funeral. More than two hundred people to whom he had given medical services sang spirituals. Clarissa Horry died the day following the death of Dr. Flagg.

UNCLE CAESAR'S DREAM

WHEN THE WAVES TURNED BACK TO THE sea and the last sounds of the wind had died away after the terrible storm of October 13, 1893, neighbors and relatives came in full force to search for the bodies of the dead. There were forty or fifty people looking for bodies, some of them from as far away as Conway. They were downcast with sorrow, and more than a few of the eyes were red-rimmed from tears.

One man explained how he aided in the search for people and property:

I gone over there 'cause they deputized anybody they got belief in. Deputize anybody with character to look for boxes and trunks and bodies. Search for all them what been drounded. We found little girl with a yellow ribbon in her hair. Gracious God. Don't want to see no more thing like that.

Plantation carpenters made pine boxes, which were placed by the sides of the roadways, and as each body was found, it was placed in a box, loaded onto a wagon, and pulled by a team of horses to a church for burial. Transporting the bodies to the churches didn't go smoothly. Fallen trees crisscrossed all roads, trails, and paths. Wood fences that had existed along some of the boundaries of the roads were down and scattered among the fallen trees and rubbish. The Reverend G. T. Wilmer, rector of All Saints Episcopal Church at Pawleys Island, conducted funerals for five consecutive days after the storm.

The search for bodies went on, but the people were unable to locate the remains of Dr. Arthur B. Flagg, the father of Dr. J. Ward Flagg, who had survived the storm by hanging onto a cedar tree. Dr. J. Ward Flagg, disconsolate over the loss of his family, was unable to assist in the search.

Caesar Chisholm, whom the people in and around Murrells Inlet called "Uncle Caesar," was especially concerned over Dr. Flagg's body. On the second night after the storm, after two days of intense searching, Uncle Caesar, full of fatigue and at the same time troubled over the lost body, threw himself on his bed. He didn't take time to remove the out-of-shape, floppy straw hat which he wore nearly all the time. The wide brim at the back was caught between the head and the mattress, but the front pulled away from the forehead. The old man's white hair made his face look jet black. In a moment, his mouth opened a little and his breathing became steady. During his slumber, Uncle Caesar had a dream to which he would refer the rest of his life as a vision.

In the dream, the man saw a portion of Dr. Flagg's body. Although only the midsection was visible, Caesar had no hesitation in identifying the body as that of Dr. Flagg. A part of the vest that had hung onto one of Dr. Flagg's arms during the storm was still there, and the watch fob, so familiar to all who knew Dr. Flagg, was hanging from a vest pocket. The flesh of the body was much swollen, but there were no cuts apparent or bruises from the effect of any blows.

In his dream, Caesar looked around frantically, trying to pinpoint the location of the body. To be sure, it was on the banks of a marsh, but there were so many marshlands in the vicinity. A wild magnolia tree emerged in the background. On the limbs were white blotches that ap-

peared to be magnolia blossoms, but then one of them flew from the tree, and it was clear that they were shore birds. Since Uncle Caesar believed the tree to be the one near the Lachicotte Swash between Murrells Inlet and Pawleys Island, the dream produced an intense excitement in his mind and roused him from sleep. For the remainder of the night he lay on his bed, his eyes staring into the darkness but seeing the midpart of Dr. Flagg's body in the Lachicotte Swash.

When dawn came, Caesar ran from his room to the porch. He grabbed a walking stick leaning against the wall and walked quickly toward the sea, where he hoped to find a searching party. The walking stick dug into the wet sand with each step.

A search for Dr. Flagg's body had already been started at the tideline, and before Caesar reached the people gathered there, he screamed, "I know where he be." He waved the walking stick in the air as he approached the men. "Doc Flagg dressed in he vest and he watch fob be in the Lasheyco Swash!"

"How is this known, Uncle Caesar?" a man who lived on Brookgreen Plantation asked.

Nearly breathless from the walk, Caesar forced himself to talk. He inhaled deeply as he spoke.

"That not 'hear say.' I have vision. Doc Flagg be dead. Him not be in bulrushes like the princess found Moses, but him be in marsh bank."

"What nonsense you talk!" a man said. Another, in an aside, muttered, "Whoever heard of such?"

Uncle Caesar continued to exclaim that he knew where the body of Dr. Flagg was, and he begged the men to accompany him to the Lachicotte Swash. Perhaps more in desperation over their fruitless attempts to find the body than in a belief of Caesar's pronouncement, they gave in.

"Proceed, Uncle Caesar," the man from Brookgreen said as he stepped aside from the group. "Show us Dr. Flagg's body."

Uncle Caesar led the way as the group walked inland from the beach and into a forest of live oaks draped in Spanish moss. With his straw hat pulled over his forehead nearly to his eyes and his walking stick digging into the mulch of the forest floor, Caesar took big, deliberate steps until the searching party had covered several miles. Then they came out into a broad expanse of open marshland.

"Uncle Caesar," the man from Brookgreen said, spreading his arms in an expansive gesture, "there's the Lachicotte Swash. Where is the body of Dr. Flagg?"

The old man's eyes took in all the men in the party. He pushed his hat back from his forehead with the tip of his walking stick. "Round 'em up," he said, beckoning everyone to come in close.

The men circled Caesar.

"Doc Flagg," Uncle Caesar began, almost as though he were making a public speech, "fight that storm hard as Gen'l Lee, Gen'l Jackson, and 'Polen Bonaparte ever fight. But Doc Flagg, he lose he battle. He body be right over there near magnolia tree."

The men ran to the marsh beyond the wild magnolia tree. Some shore birds, perching in the tree, took flight. Uncle Caesar was coming behind.

Each member of the searching party was exclusively occupied with scanning the marsh bank.

The soil of the marsh was brown, packed down by the rise and fall of two daily tides. The odor of the marsh was unmistakable. That characteristic pungency hung heavy in the air. Fiddler crabs scurried into holes in the soil.

"Look!" the man from Brookgreen said as he contemplated a spot up ahead. The others ran toward him, and they focused their eyes on something in the bank.

There was no mistake about it. The body there in the marsh was that of Dr. Flagg. Most of it was covered with marsh mud, but a piece of his vest and his familiar watch fob were plain to be seen.

The men all knelt down beside the half-buried body. Dr. Flagg's watch was ticking.

NOAH'S DOVE

ON OCTOBER 12, 1893, A YOUNG GIRL WAS VISITING her aunt on Debordieu Island. No beach house could have been simpler than her Aunt Sarah's cottage on a dune between the Atlantic Ocean and the creek that cut the island off from the mainland. Located south of Pawleys Island but north of Georgetown, Debordieu Island was sparsely settled, and no other cottages were within sight.

Early in the afternoon, the niece, Margaret, was having a conversation with her aunt when the older woman told the girl something she could hardly take in.

"I had a most remarkable dream last night," she said. "In the dream, Father came to me, as clearly as if he still lived, and said for me to gather together all the things I treasure, take them, and evacuate the island. He was so intense, just like in the old days, as he told me to take the tin box from the shelf over the window that faces the ocean and leave at once."

"What do you make of it, Aunt Sarah?" her niece asked.

"The dream?"

"Yes."

"I think . . ." Sarah began, but before she finished the sentence, her niece broke in.

"That something dreadful is going to happen?"

"Don't be rude," the aunt snapped. "You think nothing of interrupting. What on earth's the matter with your manners?"

Margaret contemplated her hands.

"Oh, I don't know," the aunt went on, dismissing her displeasure over the interruption. She got up, smoothed her skirts, and went to a window facing the sea. Even on such a muggy, gray day, her slender form was lovely. Her dress was a shade of rose, and the sleeves draped over the arms. As she turned, the dress reflected on her white skin and threw a faint blush on her face. "I'm not going to start a stampede of evacuation."

"But didn't you have a similar dream once before?" Margaret asked.

"You are the perceptive one," her aunt replied with a lilt in her voice. There was something of excitement in her, of exhilaration. "You remember that old dream?"

Margaret groaned. "Of course I remember." She removed her glasses and rubbed them on a sleeve of her dress. "Good Lord! I've heard it a thousand times. It saved your life. I'd say your dreams, at least when your father comes to you, are a bloody good protection."

"You're just like your father!"

"And you're evading the issue." Margaret put on her glasses. "Whenever I displease you, I become just like my father. Well, I never knew the gentleman, but if he believed that a spirit can come to you through a dream, then I'm with Papa."

Sarah sat down and leaned toward her niece. "Dear, there is something I have been wanting to mention to you. Your spectacles. Do you really need them? To wear them as you do most of the time, I mean?"

A sudden disturbance caused Margaret to turn her head. She got up and went to the east window. It was very hot. A little wind came in through the cracks around the window and stirred the chimes made of seashells. Their mournful, discordant sounds were a perfect background for her visit with her aunt. They had never seen eye-to-eye.

"Oh," her aunt said with a sigh. "I meant no disap-

proval. You're so youthful, and you have the magic of gracefulness. The wearing of spectacles at nineteen in no way disfigures the countenance.''

The young woman continued to look out at the dank and gloomy day. The tide was coming in now. You could hear it, although it wasn't visible because of the mist.

"Your eyes are large and gray,'' her aunt continued. ''Like mine.'' A faint smile came to her lips. ''Your hair is even better than mine,'' she added, in what seemed a kind of consolation.

Margaret turned, and the women exchanged glances. ''That former dream,'' the younger woman said, ''in which your father came to you. . . . Had you not left the island as he warned, would your situation not have been tragic?''

''My dear,'' her aunt responded, emphasizing each word, ''the Yankees were coming. They were on the march, but we were warned by servants who came from the plantation.''

''Suppose the servants had not warned you,'' Margaret said, pressing the point, ''Would you have obeyed the command of your father when he came to you in the dream and warned you to evacuate the island? Would you have left Debordieu had the servants not come to warn you of the Yankees?''

''Who can say?'' Sarah answered with a sweep of the arms. ''I don't know today what I would have done thirty years ago!'' She smiled a little, but her eyes were hard. ''I remember it well. The servants came riding up to the house just after dawn, two days after I'd had the dream in which Father ordered me to leave the island. Zack, who always took the position as leader in a group of servants, said, 'Missy, them Yankees bustin' and bangin'. More noise than enough. Terrible! Don't give no rest a-tall.' ''

''Did you leave then?''

"Yes. My goodness, yes. We left immediately for Green-ville."

"Then," the young woman goaded, "you didn't really leave as a result of the warning in the dream?"

"Why, yes; and not exactly either."

"The fact is," Margaret went on, "you wouldn't have left at all had the servants not warned you that the Yankees were on the march."

"What nonsense you talk." Sarah gave a long, steady, and contemplative look at her niece. "I don't know if that's just one of your odd notions or if it's true."

These were not the words Margaret wanted to hear. "Oh, you know you would never have left Debordieu on the basis of a dream." Her face hardened slightly as she added, "Or if you had, you would never have admitted it."

Sarah stared at her niece with frank curiosity. "I know you're young and impressionable, but why does it mean so much to you? To know whether or not I left this house on account of the dream? Let's grant that I did the best I could and acted with common sense." She walked across the room to a chest and took from it a ball of yarn and a crochet hook. Even in her most intimate moments, she never deviated from her graceful stride and good manners. "Take this and start a chain stitch. When it reaches the width you desire, I'll show you how to make a bureau scarf." She went back to the chest and took for herself a length of crocheted handwork that had been started at an earlier time. "We may as well do something constructive."

"Maybe so." Margaret absently unraveled the ball of yarn. "As you say, it may be just one of my notions. But I'm inclined not to pass off the effects of the supernatural as absurd, or with ridicule, or whatever."

"Hundreds of people in the Low Country believe in it

implicitly. The supernatural, I mean." Sarah pulled a thread through a loop with her crochet hook.

"I know that," the younger woman blurted out. "And they are not the stupid country fools you think they are."

"And more often than not," Sarah continued, not acknowledging her niece's remark, "an unexpected outcome of a prediction comes about. A result that cannot be explained by natural laws. Sometimes"—the older woman put her needlework in her lap and sat motionless for a moment—"it *does* seem more than mere coincidence."

"Oh?" breathed her niece. "Pray go on."

"Yes. Such as my former dream when Father very explicitly directed me to leave the island and take with me anything that I treasured."

"But you didn't follow his instructions until the servants came and told you the Yankees were coming. And that was two days after you'd had the dream."

The older woman surveyed her niece with pity. "I must have had dozens of dreams that could have been interpreted as warnings. Especially against something as illusionary and vague as dreams," she added in a low voice. "Do you not think we should credit ourselves with a certain intellect?"

"Perhaps it's that very intellect of which you speak that puts us at fault," Margaret said, wrapping a length of yarn around a finger heedlessly. "Such intellect, I'd say, could lull us into a false sense of security."

"Be a bit more explicit," her aunt said coolly, her crochet hook flying in and out of the intertwined loops.

"I venture to say the supernatural has certain power, immense power, and you know it. You know your father came to you in the earlier dream and warned you of danger. He came to you last night in a similar dream, with a similar warning." Margaret shook with a chill at the thought as the words tumbled out. "But you are dismissing in the name of intellect the warning that came to you last night, the same as you did before. Does it make you feel secure?"

Her aunt stood up and placed her needlework in the chair. "With the conviction that it does, I'll have Hagar bring in a pitcher of tea. . . ." "Wait." Margaret held up a hand, the palm facing her aunt. "I've decided what I'm going to do."

Sarah's lower lip twitched. "Yes?"

"I'm going to leave the island. Is Hagar's son still here? The one who met me at the dock yesterday? I'll have him row me to the mainland in his boat."

"I don't know," Sarah replied. "I'll ask Hagar if Tom is here. And I'll have her bring tea. There's nothing like a nice cup of tea . . ."

Margaret had the uncomfortable conviction that her aunt was patronizing her.

When Sarah came back into the room, she said that Tom was not in the cottage. Hagar didn't know where he was, but she assumed he was working on his boat or the fish nets, or he might be cleaning for the evening meal any fish that he had caught.

Sarah lifted her handwork from the chair and sat down. "Now, getting back to what I was saying about dreams, spirits, and the supernatural . . ."

"Oh, don't rattle on about it," Margaret flared. "You don't believe in any of it. When the Angel Gabriel blows his horn, you won't believe it!"

"You're responding with undue emotion," her aunt answered, not looking up. "Don't take on so."

Hagar pushed the door open and came in. She carried two mugs of tea, each with a piece of bread balanced on the top. Margaret hurried over to help the servant. She took a mug and handed it to her aunt. Just as Hagar hand-

ed the other mug of tea to the young woman, the servant said, "Tom not be here and that ocean gwine shake hands with the creek."

"Oh be calm," the older woman said curtly. "The tide is unusually high. That's all."

"Hagar's right," her niece cried. "A terrible storm's coming. You know it is. You were warned in the dream last night." She turned to Hagar. "The ocean may very well join the creek in a mass of water." She flexed her muscles, trying to control her trembling.

Hagar ran from the room, and Sarah turned to her niece. "Don't let Hagar's sinister warnings upset you."

The day waned. Wind gusted into a gale. The rain became a constant sheet of water, and the creek back of the house, a channel that cut Debordieu off from the mainland, churned with high swells that exploded into whitecaps of foam. The sounds of the angry ocean filled the cottage. Tom returned to the house and went into the pantry, where his mother was sitting, sipping tea. The tide was at full flood, and any opportunity for evacuation of the island had passed.

The two women worked on their handwork silently as they sat side-by-side on a settee. There was a merciful sluggishness in Margaret's mind now. Hard as she tried, she couldn't summon any feelings of boldness or bravery. The dullness had become a bulwark against the storm. She got up and spread the portion of dresser scarf that she had made on a table under the south window. "Pretty," she said quietly, letting her eyes wander around the room. "This parlor needs a little dressing up."

"Oh, dear," her aunt said in exasperation. "Beach houses are not meant to be dressed up. From time immemorial they have been plain."

"Oh?"

"Of course. You see, we come here to enjoy ourselves. We can be rather frivolous, I would say. Not so formal as we are back on the plantation, where things are dressed up."

Hagar served the evening meal to Sarah and Margaret in the parlor. Fish were served, which Tom had caught, and the meal ended with marmalade spread on thick slices of bread. As the women dined, the light of day completely disappeared, and with the darkness came a bitter chill. A cold wind blew in through the cracks around the windows.

After supper, Sarah ordered Hagar to open a bottle of sherry and bring it to the parlor. The sherry and two glasses were placed on a table near the fireplace, where the wind was bumping and roaring within the chimney walls. The older woman poured, and as she handed a glass to her niece, she said, "By morning the gale will have abated. Let's calm ourselves with a sherry and talk of something gay."

"The likes of what?"

"Let us talk about who we would like to be if we could be anyone in the world," Sarah said, as though she were familiar with such a game.

"Anyone in the world?"

"Yes. Just anyone. Who would you want to be?"

The young woman sucked her underlip in a kind of overbite as she pondered the question.

"Come on now," her aunt pressed. "Who would you choose to be?"

"I cannot think," her niece said. She circled the rim of the glass with a finger, then sipped the sherry.

"Surely you can think of lots of people you'd like to be. How about Frances Folsom Cleveland?"

"Why should I want to be Frances Cleveland?"

"I should think every woman would want to be the wife

of the president!'' her aunt exclaimed, now excited over the game. "Why would you not want to be Mrs. Cleveland?''

"Well, I hear the president stays up until three in the morning, going over every bit of official business. And I have also heard that he insists on answering the Bell telephone each time it rings at the White House. Oh, I'd never want to be his wife!''

"And you cannot think of anyone you would want to be other than yourself?''

Just then there was a slight movement of the house, and the window panes rattled as thunder boomed overhead.

"Yes. I know who I would want to be,'' Margaret answered.

"Who?''

"I'd want to be Noah!''

"Noah! That's silly.''

"No. I'd really want to be Noah. He'd just float away in his boat, and I do not know what is going to happen to us if this storm continues.''

The women sipped the sherry until their glasses were empty. The aunt refilled the glasses, and they drank again until the glasses had no wine in them. Then Sarah and her niece prepared to retire for the night. They chose to sleep in the same room and in the same bed.

In the hours that followed, Sarah talked on some of her favorite subjects, and sometime before dawn, sleep came to both the women. They were still in slumber when Hagar burst into the room, shouting.

"Gracious God, Missy, you in the bed and takin' it so easy, and the water's comin' in at the door!'' She ran from the room before her mistress could answer.

The two women lost no time in getting their clothes on. They hurried to the parlor. Hagar was nearly mad with

fear. "Tom gone to check he fish nets, Missy, and the creek and the sea be united."

Margaret ran to the east window. A fierce wind was pushing the tide toward the house. Water that had been thrown on the porch was coming in under the door.

"Get the prayer book," Sarah cried, but not waiting for someone else to do so, she grabbed it from a table. She turned a page, then another. "Drat!" she said, handing the book to her niece. "Here. You have on your spectacles. Read the prayer for those at sea."

"Kneel," Margaret suggested softly.

The three women knelt on the floor as Margaret began to read from the prayer book. Just then something crashed against the door, and a sound was heard above the roar of the tide. "Baa-a-a-a."

Hagar ran for the door.

"Don't open the door," Sarah shouted, getting up. "That's only a goat trying to get inside. If you open the door, we're gone." She ran to the east window and reached as high as she could, pulling a box from a shelf over the window. Margaret had joined her now, and Sarah cried, "Help me save this box. Some valuable documents are inside."

Hagar, her face full of fear, yet trying to dispel her mistress' terror, said, "Missy, don't be afraid. Massa Jesus at the helm."

"Look!" From the window Margaret saw a small log house that had been used for the washing and ironing of clothes floating by.

"Oh, my god!" Hagar cried. "My nice new lantern I just done buy, and all the clothes!"

"Let us all sing together 'Jesus, Lover of My Soul,' " Sarah said. The women sang the words of the hymn with as much strength as they could summon. Sarah's eyes were closed, and she held the box she had taken from the shelf.

Suddenly, the water turned and started back toward the sea. Hagar ran for the door.

"Tom," she said. "Gotta find Tom."

"Stop!" the older woman called. "Wait. The water may be too high to open the door."

"But no water comin' in round the cracks," Hagar reasoned.

"Open the door just slightly," Sarah ordered. "Just a crack."

The servant pulled the door open only about an inch or two. A white bird fluttered its way in.

Margaret ran to the door, took the bird in her hand, and smoothed its wet, soggy feathers.

"Nora's dove," Hagar said.

"Yes," the young woman said. "It really is Noah's dove."

Hagar pushed the door open. It was cold and dim, and a part of the porch had been washed away. She looked across the beach, which was nearly covered in seashells, seaweed, chunks of foam, splintered wood, and a thousand other things. Tom was staggering toward the house. Before he reached his mother, he screamed that he had survived the storm by lying on the peak of a high dune and hanging on to some wild olive bushes that were growing there.

UNCLE HARDTIMES AND MOM PLEASANT

A Folktale

UNCLE HARDTIMES WAS A GATEKEEPER. EACH DAY AS he opened and closed the gate, he greeted the people as they passed through.

Uncle Hardtimes had no money. One day as he stood at the gate, looking through the avenue of trees at the white-columned manor house, he thought about how poor he was. And he thought about how rich his master was. He tried to work out a plan to get some money.

One morning soon afterwards, when the master came riding down the avenue on his fine stallion named Stocking Foot, Hardtimes motioned for him to stop. The master pulled on the reins and stopped Stocking Foot.

"Cap'n," the old gatekeeper said.

"Yes, Uncle Hardtimes?"

"I'm in trouble." Uncle Hardtimes was not really in trouble. He just wanted the master to think that he was.

"What is the trouble?" the master asked.

"I lost Mom Pleasant last night," Uncle Hardtimes said.

"You lost Mom Pleasant? Your wife died last night?" the master asked.

"Yes," Uncle Hardtimes said. He dropped his head and looked at the ground and dug a toe into the sand. "Please, Cap'n," he sobbed, "let me have twenty-five dollars to put Mom Pleasant away right."

"Is that enough to bury Mom Pleasant?"

"Yes, Cap'n."

The master gave the old man twenty-five dollars and then flapped the reins in the air and rode through the gate.

Uncle Hardtimes was so excited he couldn't wait to tell Mom Pleasant. He ran through the grove of oaks to a row of cabins where the workers on the plantation lived. His cabin was about midway in the row of small houses.

"Pleasant! Pleasant!" Uncle Hardtimes called as he ran through the street.

"That you, Hardtimes?" Mom Pleasant called from inside the cabin.

"It's me all right."

Mom Pleasant ran to the porch.

"Pleasant, ole gal, I got us some money," Uncle Hardtimes said, holding the money out for his wife to see.

"How did you get it?" Mom Pleasant wiped her hands on her apron.

"I told the Cap'n you were dead. If you see him comin', you'd better play dead."

Uncle Hardtimes and Mom Pleasant talked about the money. They had never had twenty-five dollars at one time in their lives. They decided to go to the country store and buy some things they had wanted to buy but had never had the money with which to buy them.

They went to the store and bought vittles and yards of cloth, and that night they had the best supper they had ever eaten.

The next morning, Mom Pleasant took her hoe and started walking to the cotton field. On the sandy lane leading to the field she saw her missus riding her mare. A thought came to Mom Pleasant about how she could get some more money. She waved her hands and called to her missus to stop. "Missus!"

"Yes?" the missus replied as her mare pranced to a stop.

"I lost Hardtimes last night," Mom Pleasant said as she dropped her head and looked at the sandy earth under her bare feet. She was trying to appear to be sad.

"You mean Uncle Hardtimes is dead?" the missus asked.

"That's right," Mom Pleasant answered. "I need twenty-five dollars to put him away right."

The missus lifted a bag attached to the saddle. She took some money from the bag. "Is twenty-five dollars enough, Mom Pleasant?"

"Yes, ma'am. That's enough. That'll put him away nice."

The missus rode away on her mare, and Mom Pleasant was so excited about her good fortune she hurried home to tell Hardtimes before he left to go to the gate at the avenue of oaks. "I got twenty-five dollars," she said. "I told the missus you were dead and I needed twenty-five dollars to put you away nice."

Uncle Hardtimes and Mom Pleasant laughed about the joke they had played on their master and missus. Then they went back to the country store and bought more of the good things they had gotten the day before.

That night the missus told her husband that Uncle Hardtimes was dead and she had given Mom Pleasant twenty-five dollars with which to bury him.

The master looked straight at his wife. "You must be mistaken. Uncle Hardtimes isn't dead. Mom Pleasant is the one who died. I gave Uncle Hardtimes twenty-five dollars with which to bury her."

"No," the missus said. "I saw Mom Pleasant today and she asked me for twenty-five dollars for the burial expenses."

The missus and master decided to ride over to the cabin of Uncle Hardtimes and Mom Pleasant and see just which

51

one of them had died. Two horses were hooked to a carriage, and the missus and master rode along the avenue of oaks and down the lane until they came to the row of cabins.

Mom Pleasant and Uncle Hardtimes were finishing an even better supper than the one they had had the night before when they heard the carriage stop in the yard. Uncle Hardtimes looked out the window and said, "As sure as my name is Hardtimes, that's the Cap'n."

Mom Pleasant jumped up and went to the window. "And the missus is with him!"

"You fall down and be dead," Uncle Hardtimes yelled to his wife.

"You be dead, too," she yelled back. "As dead as a fat 'possum."

When the master and missus came into the cabin, both Uncle Hardtimes and Mom Pleasant were lying on the floor. Their eyes were closed, and they were pretending to be dead.

The master looked at his wife and winked.

"I'd give twenty-five dollars to the one who died first if I knew who that was. But since I do not know which one of them died first, I will just keep the twenty-five dollars," the master said.

Uncle Hardtimes and Mom Pleasant jumped up at the very same time, each of them saying, "I died first!"

THE MAN WHO HID IN THE CHIMNEY

THERE CAN BE NO COUGHING OR RUSTLING OF LEAVES now, the young slave man thought. Somewhere in the forest of live oaks and pine trees, near the plantation property line, two white patrollers were roaming in the night. They were Raw Head and Bloody Bones, the most dreaded of all the patrollers on Low Country plantations. They were equipped with hound dogs that had been trained to detect the foot scent and track down any person in the forest.

The man was making his way toward the property line, which he planned to cross in order to visit a girl who lived on an adjoining plantation. He could have obtained a pass from the master of the plantation, which would have given him permission to cross the property line. But he hadn't taken the time from his task in the rice fields to go to the master and request the pass. He had thought about getting a pass, during the day, but it hadn't seemed so important then. Now, he wished he had a pass. It was common knowledge that when Raw Head and Bloody Bones apprehended a slave crossing a property line without a pass, they whipped him with a plaited, cowhide whip until blood ran from the wounds.

A whispered word and the sounds of dry sticks breaking made the man realize that Raw Head and Bloody Bones were nearby and that they would surely track him down.

He must run back to the plantation and find a place to hide. But where could he hide that the patrollers and their dogs would not find him? His mother's cabin? The barn?

As he darted wildly through the trees, he visualized his mother in the cabin and thought of the brutish treatment she would likely receive from the patrollers if she attempted to hide him. But the barn was on the far side of the cabins; he couldn't possibly reach the barn and hide there. His mother's cabin was the only place he could go, even though he was risking cruel behavior toward his mother.

"They're comin'. Hide me quick," the man said to his mother as he ran in.

"Who comin'?"

"Raw Head and Bloody Bones. Hide me quick!"

The woman's eyes searched the room. She ran to a barrel and moved it slightly, then moved it back. Inside the barrel would surely be the first place the patrollers would look.

"Great God in the mornin'," she said. "I don't know what they want to carry on like that for." She looked at the bedstead with a mattress made of corn shucks. No place to hide there.

"I don't want to get busted up," the man said.

"Why didn't you fix your mind on gettin' a pass from Massa?" the mother asked, her eyes darting around the room as she tried to locate a place where her son could conceal himself.

"I didn't think in that way," he answered. "I just be gone long 'nuf to see gal name Lessie. But them patrollers saw me when I was on the blossom end of a footlog and them on the butt end. Hide me quick or they'll whip me 'til they can put me in their pocket."

The woman's eyes were still searching the room. When they came to the fireplace, they stopped moving. "Up the chimney," she ordered.

The son backed into the fireplace, then raised his head inside the chimney. The chimney was made of brick and was of rectangular shape, but as the man looked up, it appeared to be a black cylinder.

"Up your foots!" the mother commanded.

The son seized some projection above his head and pulled himself upward, but his legs dangled in full view.

"Up your foots!" the woman cried as she ran to the fireplace. She squatted down and began to push her son's feet. "Up," she said. "Go."

Resting his naked toes on protruding pieces of mortar, the son ascended until a foot slipped and some pieces of mortar fell down into the fireplace. He wriggled himself back up until he seized a protruding brick from which he could pull himself higher.

As soon as her son's feet were out of sight, the woman grabbed a broom and started sweeping the room.

"COME OUT!" Raw Head shouted, in the midst of a loud clatter on the porch. The dogs growled and snarled at the door leading into the room.

"We know you're in there," Bloody Bones called as a leather whip snapped in the air and rang out in the night like a report from a shotgun.

"Who you lookin' for?" the woman called from the room as she brushed the floor with the broom.

"Your son, that's who," Raw Head said, throwing open the door.

"He not be here," the woman answered, trying for all the world to conceal her fear of the patrollers.

"He may be slick, but he's not that slick," Raw Head said. He marched into the room as Bloody Bones held the dogs back with his whip. Raw Head walked over to the barrel and looked inside.

"He not be here," the woman said.

Bloody Bones came inside the room, closing the door

behind him, blocking out the dogs which were trying to come into the room. Bloody Bones went straight to the bedstead and cracked his whip on the mattress. When he realized the son was not hiding under the mattress, he seemed agitated. "Tell that pea head," he said in a voice soft with sarcasm, "if he doesn't come out, we'll beat him 'til he'll have to use the meat in his rations to grease his back with." He walked by the woman, pushing her aside with the handle of his whip. Bloody Bones then kicked the leg of a table, and the woman, still holding to her broom, recoiled.

Just then a few pieces of mortar fell into the fireplace. "Oh, Lordy," the woman muttered before she could restrain herself.

Raw Head and Bloody Bones eyed the fireplace, then the woman.

"Any fire in the fireplace tonight?" Raw Head asked.

"No," the woman answered.

"Anything *else* in the fireplace tonight?" Bloody Bones questioned.

"No."

"I 'spect somethin's in the fireplace." Raw Head gave a wicked grin.

"Reckon so," Bloody Bones said. "I hear tell some folks cures their meat in the fireplace."

"A side 'o beef's sometimes hung in the chimney to cure," Raw Head added.

"If there's meat in this fireplace," Bloody Bones went on, "I'd sorta like to have some."

Raw Head reflected for a moment, then held the cowhide whip by the handle and let the whip dangle in the air. "Why don't we have the gal here build a fire and cure the meat a little?"

Bloody Bones grinned widely. There were no teeth in his upper gum. "Where's your woodpile, gal?"

"Porch," the woman answered, barely loud enough to be heard.

Bloody Bones went to the porch. The dogs stopped growling and looked at him. He came back into the room with an armload of twigs to be used as kindling, and some limbs of scrub oak.

The mother of the man in the chimney held out trembling arms in a gesture to stop the effort to build a fire in the fireplace. Bloody Bones dumped the wood into her arms, and she nearly fell from the weight of the wood.

"Step it up," Raw Head said, indicating with a movement of the whip to get the fire going. "Gal, you'd better quit messin' around."

The woman knelt down and stacked the kindling twigs crosswise and put the scrub oak on top of the twigs. She stood up and did not turn around for a moment. Then she turned, and there was an expression of relief in her eyes. "I don't have no fire."

"We'll get fire," Bloody Bones said. He went to the porch and called to the people in the adjoining cabin, telling them to fetch some fire.

In a few minutes a woman came to the cabin. She held her arms straight in front of her as she carried a hot coal between two sticks.

Bloody Bones, still on the porch, held the dogs back as the woman came inside.

"Start the fire," Raw Head snapped at her.

The woman dropped the hot coal into the fireplace and with a stick pushed it under the twigs. She hurried from the cabin.

In a few seconds, a finger of fire curled around a twig. Then another shot upward. In a moment the fireplace was ablaze with fire, and heat spread into the room. The mother eased herself into a chair and began to cry.

"Quit that sniffin'," Bloody Bones said. He pulled a

chair away from the table and sat down. "We'll just sit a spell and let that meat cure."

The fire cracked and popped, and the mother of the man in the chimney dissolved in tears. Raw Head jolted her with the handle of the lash. "I thought we told you to stop that sniffin'."

All of a sudden someone stepped on the porch, and the dogs went into a frenzy of barking and growling. The door flew open, and the woman's son lurched into the room.

"Who's that?" Raw Head asked, although it was perfectly clear who it was.

"Well, it ain't no spirit," Bloody Bones answered.

The woman's son took a crumpled paper from his pocket and handed it to Raw Head. "That be my pass," he said.

"Where'd you get this?" Raw Head asked.

"From the Massa. You can't whip me now 'cause I got my pass. Signed by the Massa."

"You climbed up the chimney, crawled out on the roof, and jumped off to go and see the Master?" Bloody Bones asked, looking over Raw Head's shoulder at the paper.

"Must've" Raw Head added. "That must be what he done."

"You can't whip me now," the man insisted. "Massa said him got to do best by me and he sign my pass."

The patrollers shook their heads. They couldn't whip him now. He had a pass.

THE CASE OF THE HEADLESS CORPSE

RHETT CEMETERY, ON A BLUFF OVERLOOKING PORT Royal Sound, was veiled in gray anonymity on a Friday in November, 1979. Granite headstones were accentuated by the misty darkness. Toward evening, Abraham Burns, a member of the Third Macedonia Baptist Church, who helped care for the cemetery, walked into the burial ground looking for firewood. As he strolled between two rows of ancient oaks, then over to the woods, he noticed a large mound silhouetted against the steadily increasing blackness. A few steps more and he was enveloped in a macabre dream world. Hex dolls with pins sticking in them swayed from overhanging limbs. Corncobs, decorated with bows fashioned of ribbon, hung from trees draped in Spanish moss. Dirt was piled up to the side of a gaping hole, and the top of a closed coffin was exposed to the night. Slips of paper with written curses were scattered on the mound of dirt that had been dug away from the grave.

"I didn't recognize anything," Burns said later. "The [coffin's] top was still on. There were maybe one or two tracks in the pile of dirt, not too many."

The coffin in the grave presumably held the body of Norman Middleton, Sr., who had been killed eight months earlier when he was struck by some heavy machinery on the back of a pickup truck. A coroner's jury conducted an investigation of the accident but declined to bring criminal

charges against the truck driver. Middleton's body contained .30 percent alcohol, three times as much as would have been necessary to convict him had he been driving. Moreover, he had escaped death in an earlier accident when he was struck by a car while walking intoxicated on a highway.

After Middleton's death, his sons, Norman, Jr., and Weldon, of Savannah, sued Charles Barnard, the driver, and Nicholas Meyer, the owner of the truck, for $500,000. The lawsuit was settled out of court for $23,000, and the settlement was filed in the courthouse about a week before the evening that Burns walked into Rhett Cemetery.

"I was thinking the family knew about this; but later I decided to call someone," Burns said. On hearing the news that their father's grave had been violated, Norman and Weldon Middleton, through a lawyer, had a court order issued simultaneously to the Beaufort County sheriff's department and the Wright Donaldson Funeral Home. The document ordered that the coffin be opened and the body examined.

Acting quickly, and perhaps without thinking that he might be destroying evidence the sheriff's department would consider important, William Marshall of the Wright Donaldson Funeral Home already had the top of the coffin removed when investigators from the sheriff's department arrived. The body of Middleton was there, but the head had been cut off and taken away.

"What was curious to me," G. R. Wagner, a lieutenant in the detective division, said when the sheriff's detective went to work on the strange case, "was that it was within a week after the settlement of the lawsuit that the tragic incident of opening up the gentleman's grave was found." The family of the victim requested that the detectives refrain from discussing the case with outsiders when reporters from the *New York Times,* the *Boston Globe*, and other big-city newspapers arrived in Beaufort to cover the story. Investigators agreed to cooperate with the family in that respect, but they had no leads in the case and welcomed any help they could get.

They called in J. E. McTeer, of Coffin's Point Plantation in Frogmore, South Carolina, the very heart of the voodoo belt. McTeer was a former sheriff of Beaufort County and a witch doctor himself. He claimed that his mother and grandmother had been gifted with extrasensory perception and that he had inherited their talent. His grandmother, Louisa Guerard Heyward, was the wife of a rice planter and had observed slaves brought from Africa. She studied their use of hexes and spells, and she didn't overlook slave secrets some people scorned.

When his family bought a four-hundred-acre farm in 1912, McTeer, then nine, met Aunt Emmeline and Uncle Tony. Their parents had been slaves, and they spoke Gullah. Uncle Tony practiced voodoo and talked with spirits. The boy learned some of the old man's secrets.

McTeer's father, sheriff of Beaufort County, died in 1926, and the governor appointed the son to fill his late father's post. He was, at twenty-two, the youngest sheriff in the nation. He had become well known for his knowledge and practice of root medicine, spells, and witchcraft, and after he was sworn into office, he became actively involved in the practice of witchcraft. He saw people dying, going crazy, shooting each other, and in an effort to help them, he conducted magical ceremonies, often using plastic dolls, floating skulls, cemetery dirt, and horseshoe crabs. During the time he served as sheriff, he sometimes joined forces with Dr. Buzzard, a witch doctor of national fame, in order to solve crimes committed in Beaufort County. McTeer estimated that more than five thousand people came to him for help after he became involved in the supernatural.

In McTeer's opinion, the decapitation in Rhett Cemetery

was the work of voodoo cultists. Somebody familiar with the victim's funeral led the perpetrator to the grave, and the crime was committed by somebody outside Beaufort County, maybe Savannah or New York. "Down in the Caribbean they use that sort of thing profusely," McTeer said. "This is a true case of black magic. Someone is trying to put evil on the people connected with him [the victim]."

King Oseijeman Adefunmi of the African Yoruba Village in Sheldon, fifteen miles north of Beaufort, said he suspected sorcery. He had been initiated into the Orisha-Voodoo priesthood in Cuba. He said the beheading of a corpse is a common ritual among Cuban sorcerers, who believe it can be used to summon the dead man's spirit. According to Adefunmi, the skull of a corpse may also be used to capture evil spirits to make them do your bidding. The skull may be placed in a small iron pot, or "caldera," to which animal bones are added. Priests at the African village twenty minutes from Rhett Cemetery use ancient ritual but only to benefit others, the African high priest said.

Soon after the exhumation unexplained incidents began to happen. One of Middleton's lawyers, Tom Jessee, became strangely ill the day after getting the exhumation order. Pictures of the grave taken by the sheriff's department came back blank.

And then, another strange thing happened. At least there are those who still wonder if there is a connection to the case. On December 29, 1979, less than one month after he had been consulted, J. E. McTeer died at Beaufort Memorial Hospital of emphysema and pneumonia. He was seventy-six.

The officers of the Beaufort County sheriff's department go about their work, these days, with a perfect suavity.

62

They say the case has not been solved, but is it possible they know something we do not know?

At least one person employed by the Beaufort County sheriff's department believes in witchcraft to the extent that she carries in her purse an amulet made by a witch doctor. Amulets consist of bones, roots, herbs, and other items held within a red felt bag. The witch doctor who prepared this amulet called it a hex root, and he said in order to render a hex root potent he had to place a hand at the base of the brain of the person who would carry the amulet. "That is where electric emanations flow . . . and there our forces are joined." He also explained that people carrying his amulets will be protected from evil spirits as long as they keep the hex roots with them.

But what about the person or persons who committed the crime in Rhett Cemetery? It is believed by hundreds of Low Country men that anyone who tampers with a burial mound or a dead body buried in a grave will be punished in a most dreadful way by the spirit of the dead person who was buried in the desecrated grave. But could the perpetrator of this hideous crime also be protected by the powers of an amulet? Which spell, then, would have the greater force? The spirit of the dead person or the power of the amulet?

Could it be, then, that the officers who go about their work pleasantly, smiling, rely on the belief that the spirit of the dead penalizes in some horrible way those who tamper with a burial mound? And could it be that the officers expect the spirit of the dead man to punish the guilty party or parties in some dreadful way, thereby exposing the guilty party and solving the crime?

Or has it already happened?

THE GOLD-WATCHER

IN 1930, AT A TIME WHEN THE PEOPLE OF THE SOUTH Carolina Low Country were unable to find jobs, a sleek, white yacht pulled alongside a pier in the Georgetown harbor. Members of the crew jumped from the yacht and tied the vessel to the pier. The owner of the yacht came ashore. He was more than six feet in height, and he was attired in the best suit and leather shoes that the tailors and shoemakers of London could fashion. Although he was American, he bought his clothes in England. As he walked onto Georgetown's main street, he carried a walking stick with a handle of gold.

The man was Archer Milton Huntington, the only son of Collis P. Huntington, who had been one of the country's twelve richest men. Collis had owned the Central Pacific Railroad and had founded the Newport News Shipbuilding Company. It seemed to outsiders that he had been able to obtain by one means or another everything he desired except one thing: a son. At the age of sixty-three he married a widow from Alabama. She had a fourteen-year-old son, Archer. Huntington adopted Archer and gave him his name.

Those who knew the elder Huntington said he felt that he had fathered a son; none could have been more suited to his expectations than Archer. The youngster's energy seemed unlimited, and his quick mind grasped everything he saw and read. Consequently, it was a shattering experience for Collis P. Huntington, who had spent his life acquiring one of the country's greatest fortunes, when his

son told him that he intended to spend his life giving it away.

During his visit to Georgetown, Archer Huntington's interest in wildlife and sculpture led him to buy four adjoining plantations: The Oaks, Springfield, Laurel Hill, and Brookgreen. On the properties he planned to construct an outdoor museum for the plants and trees native to the region and to display among them the sculpture executed by his wife, Anna. Anna and Archer Huntington continued their trip to the West Indies, but when they returned to their plantations in Murrells Inlet, they were well along with the plans for their outdoor museum, to be named Brookgreen Gardens.

When word spread that a millionaire was starting an outdoor museum, there was a great scramble for jobs. Most of those living on the back roads didn't have regular work. When they earned a few dollars, they looked at them, and counted them, and figured out how far they would go. They didn't go very far. There was no such thing as new clothes. You were thankful to have a warm place in the winter and food for the table.

A man named Joe went to a physician in the community and requested the doctor to go to Huntington in his behalf and ask him to find a job for Joe.

Joe was introduced to Huntington, who was busy making plans for a winter home for himself and his wife. Huntington talked with a construction foreman, and Joe was given a job loading sand on a truck and removing it from the site of the future house.

The first day on the job, Joe carefully loaded sand onto the truck. Unaware that Huntington was watching him, he started the motor and moved the truck away from the big hole from which the sand had been taken. Just then the brakes on the truck failed and the vehicle rammed into a

tree. Huntington stormed up to the wreckage and fired Joe on the spot.

Joe was devastated. He needed work. His family was in need of food and clothing and a more substantial house than the one in which they were living. Since this was the time of the Great Depression, it was unlikely that he could find employment elsewhere.

Joe sent word to Huntington that he wanted to talk with him. As Huntington never consulted with anyone for any length of time without an appointment, a time was set for the meeting. Joe asked for his job back. Huntington told Joe he would consider his request and would let him know at the end of two weeks. At that time Joe was given a job. But it was a tough time for him, since Huntington and some of the construction foremen seemed slow to forget the accident.

Joe worked hard. He tried his best to gain the confidence and respect of the millionaire. When the Christmas holidays arrived, Huntington sent for Joe. He gave him two dollars and said, "Don't buy a car with it."

The house was completed and named Atalaya, meaning tower in the sand. Joe was given the job of keeping wood stacked by the fireplaces. There were twenty-five fireplaces in the dwelling, including a fireplace in each of the bathrooms. There was plenty of oak wood, as huge oaks were being cut during the construction of Brookgreen Gardens. Joe split logs, stacked wood, and kept fires burning in the rooms. He began to think that he had gained the confidence of Mrs. Huntington, but he still wasn't sure how her husband felt about him. Could it be that the man still held against him the fact that the brakes on the truck had failed and that he had crashed into a tree?

During this time there were rumors that Huntington hoarded large quantities of money at Atalaya. No one

seemed to know where the money came from, where it went, or even what form of legal tender Huntington preferred. Was it paper? Or silver? Was it possible that he stockpiled gold coins? According to rumormongers in the hallways of Atalaya, Huntington received about $80,000 per day in income on his investments, and he had given his wife $10 million to use in the construction of Brookgreen Gardens as a setting for her sculpture. If the fortune was indeed at Atalaya, Joe saw none of it. He attended the fireplaces and thought little of anything so unlikely as a large quantity of money in the mansion.

One day Mrs. Huntington sent for Joe. She told him she was preparing to carve a statue of Don Quixote, the hero of the novel by Cervantes. She needed an especially scrawny horse to be used as a model. She asked Joe to find her such a horse.

He went into the countryside and found a nag that apparently was dying. Its bones showed clearly through its rough coat, and its head hung nearly to its knees. Foam dropped from the horse's mouth. Joe obtained the horse from the owner and led it to the courtyard of Atalaya. Mrs. Huntington was delighted with the selection of the animal. Such a horse was just what she desired for her model. She committed herself to nurse it back to health as she worked on her sculpture. And surely Mrs. Huntington was pleased with Joe for finding her such a horse. He asked her to let him clean the animal's stable each day, and she assigned him the task.

When a man came to see Joe and told him that Huntington wanted to see him in his office, Joe was concerned. Had he done something that displeased the millionaire? What was the purpose of the confrontation? Joe left Atalaya and went to Brookgreen, where Huntington now had an office. Huntington told Joe to meet him at the bathroom on the south side of Atalaya at dusk. ''Yes, sir,''

Joe answered, not inquiring as to the nature of the assignment.

Just as the sun went down, Joe went to the bathroom to meet Huntington. He stacked heart-of-pine kindling in the fireplace and put oak logs on top of it. As soon as he touched the kindling with a match, it burst into flame. Joe sat on the floor by the fireplace to await his employer.

In a few minutes, Joe heard noises in the hallway. The hallways at Atalaya were of brick, as Huntington preferred to build his mansions of masonry rather than carry insurance to replace them in case of fire. The floors of the hallway were brick as well as the walls and ceiling. Joe ran to the bathroom door and looked into the passageway. Huntington was rolling a table toward him. Joe hurried to assist him and pulled with all his strength until the table had been moved into the bathroom. As the glowing fire reflected on the table, the table itself seemed about to burst into flame. For there, on the table, were stacks of gold, real gold, coins. The size of the coins varied from that of a watermelon seed to that of a silver dollar.

"Joe," Huntington said, "since it is necessary for me to keep the gold here in the house tonight, I want you to remain here in the bathroom and keep an eye on it. I will come for it in the morning."

During the hours that followed, Joe sat by the fire, seldom taking his eyes off the gold before him. As the sun came over the Atlantic, Huntington came to the bathroom. He thanked Joe and told him he could go to his home and rest. Huntington rolled the table of gold from the bathroom and down the hallway.

Whatever doubt Joe had had about Huntington respecting him vanished never to return. For the millionaire to have trusted Joe with the gold, which Joe thought must be absolutely pure gold, was to have ultimate faith in him. If Huntington had thought for a minute that Joe would have

pocketed the smallest coin, he would never have given him the task of watching the gold.

To this day, Joe doesn't know where the gold came from or where it went. He only knows that it was there that night and that Huntington gave him the task of guarding it. And he knows that the job that started out so badly ended with each man respecting, even liking, the other.

DR. BUZZARD'S COFFIN

THE JAILHOUSE IN OLD BEAUFORT WAS DARK AND sour and not the cleanest place in the world.

A jailer and three policemen were getting ready to lock Dr. Buzzard in a coffin. Dr. Buzzard, a nationally famous witch doctor of Beaufort, South Carolina, had asked them to lock him in a coffin so that he could give irrefutable evidence of his power in witchcraft and voodoo. He claimed that if the officers used every chain and lock at their disposal in an effort to hold him in the coffin, his escape would be testimony to the power of his black magic.

The officers both feared and respected Dr. Buzzard, as did the hundreds of people who came to him to be treated in his practice of witchcraft. They vowed they would lock him in the coffin so securely it would be impossible for him to escape.

A coffin was brought to the old jail. Dr. Buzzard climbed in and settled himself down. The jailer asked him if he was ready for the top to be closed. Dr. Buzzard asked what time it was. The jailer pulled a watch from a pocket by a chain. "It's eleven o'clock."

"Then I'll eat dinner with Mama and the boy at the usual time—one o'clock," Dr. Buzzard said.

Just then the jailer had second thoughts. "Are you sure you want to go through with this, Dr. Buzzard? Much as I want to stop your practice of witchcraft, I don't want to kill you."

"How many times have you brought me before the bar of justice?" Dr. Buzzard asked.

"Several," the jailer answered.

"And every time you thought you had an airtight case against me," the man in the coffin snapped.

"Yep."

"Then this case," Dr. Buzzard said, spreading his hands to indicate the coffin, "isn't airtight either. Close the top before I put a hex on you!"

The jailer slammed the top down. The last thing in the world anyone in Beaufort would want would be a hex inflicted on him by Dr. Buzzard.

The three policemen wrapped a chain around the coffin and pulled the ends together as tightly as they could. At the center of the coffin, on the top, they hooked the ends with a lock and snapped the lock shut. To the left and right of the middle chain, other chains were pulled together and fastened with locks. The jailer dropped the keys to the locks into his breast pocket and patted his pocket. The other men laughed. They left the jailhouse and went down the street to eat lunch in a tavern on the banks of Port Royal Sound.

As the jailer and policemen dined on crab cakes and coffee, they talked about Dr. Buzzard and how he had acquired the gift, or the "mantle," as he called it, of dealing with the supernatural from his father, the original Dr. Buzzard.

The first Dr. Buzzard came to Beaufort on a slave ship. Almost as soon as he was given a cabin in which to live, his master learned of his magical powers. This Dr. Buzzard had so much influence over the other slaves that his master gave him a large measure of freedom to be used in the practice of witchcraft. When the slaves were allowed to pursue their ancestral customs and beliefs, they performed their tasks more cheerfully.

The people born in slavery and their descendants relied on those who "worked in root" for their medical needs.

Roots were mixed with cemetery dirt, frogs' feet, hearts of owls, and crushed bones and used as charms.

As slaves slipped across property lines and came to the original Dr. Buzzard for treatment, his son, the man in the coffin, learned many of his father's secrets. When his father became too old and sickly to practice, the son took over the work. He wore purple eyeglasses, a custom which prevented others from seeing his eyes, and he seemed to be always chewing on a root. The root on which he chewed had magical power, according to Dr. Buzzard. He said if he went into a courtroom during the time a case was being tried, he could chew the root and affect the outcome of the case. He also used another procedure in affecting the result of trials. He concocted a powder by grinding together certain materials, and he sprinkled the powder on desks, tables, and chairs in the courtroom. After the powder had been scattered about the courtroom, Dr. Buzzard said the room had been "rooted," and the course of the trial in progress would change.

Dr. Buzzard's routine also called for the use of black cats. He said there was no stronger force in the world than that of a bone from a black cat that had been boiled *alive*! The technique called for Dr. Buzzard to put a black cat in a kettle of boiling water, and when the hot water covered the cat, "That cat would talk just like a man."

After the cat had been boiled, it was dropped into a sack (the water in which the cat had been boiled was poured into a container for future use, as it was considered to be powerful in the treatment of certain maladies) and taken to a creek. The cooked cat was then dumped into the creek. If the process of boiling the cat and dumping the remains into the creek had been done correctly, according to the unexplained techniques of voodoo, all the bones would float away from the bank of the creek or sink, except

one bone. "That bone just floats right to me," Dr. Buzzard said. That was the bone with the power. Anyone carrying that bone was safe from "the law and everything else."

Dr. Buzzard also worked with snakes. He captured rattlesnakes from the woods and fields and gave them names. One snake's name was Sam. When Dr. Buzzard used Sam in a cure, he would say, "Come here, Sam," and have the patient lie still while the serpent slid over him.

According to Root Man, a son of Dr. Buzzard, and also a witch doctor who practices the magical and mystical art of witchcraft and voodooism in the manner of his father, some members of the police force had shot at Dr. Buzzard on several occasions. It wasn't uncommon for fugitives to make their way to Dr. Buzzard's house in order to have a hex put on someone, or to have a hex removed, or to avail themselves of one of Dr. Buzzard's remedies. During these times, law enforcement officers often showed up and confronted not only the fugitives but Dr. Buzzard as well. On several occasions, a shoot-out had resulted from the fracas. "But my daddy just caught them bullets and threw them right back to the police," Root Man said.

When the officers and the jailer had concluded their meal, they walked quickly back to the jailhouse. Each of them held a toothpick in his mouth and even carried on his part of the conversation without losing control of the toothpick.

"What if Dr. Buzzard couldn't get out of the coffin?" a policeman asked. "He might be gettin' pretty blue in the face 'bout now."

The jailer transferred his toothpick from one side of his mouth to the other as he said, "Seems to me there's plenty who wouldn't mind if he never got out of that box. Anyway, I for one don't want to be under his evil influence.

You heard him say if I didn't close the coffin he'd put a hex on me."

"Hurry," one of the officers behind him said. "We shouldn't have left the old man so long."

They rushed into the room, their hearts beating feverishly. And then they stopped. No ordinary phenomenon could have excited such sensations as they felt.

The chains that had been pulled around the coffin and locked together were scattered about the floor. The jailer ran to the coffin and lifted the top. A black cat jumped out.

"Beats me," the jailer said, shaking his head.

"You can see Dr. Buzzard, and you can believe in him," an officer muttered, "but you sure can't explain him."

LIJA'S GIFT OF PROPHESY

A Folktale

LIJA, A BUTLER, WAS LIKE THE MAN WHO WENT TO the reading of a relative's will and found out that he had been left a huge legacy. He thought he might figure in something important, but he hadn't the remotest idea of how enormous it would turn out to be.

When Lija became interested in one of the cooks in the outside-the-house plantation kitchen, he frequently stuck his head in the door to see her. While chatting with the cook, Lija would sneak a glance at the food bubbling in the pots.

One day Lija met his master in the yard and said, "Boss, sho as you is born, I can tell you what you gwine eat for breakfast."

"What am I going to eat for breakfast?" the master asked.

"You gwine have hominy, eggs, ham, coffee, and biscuits," Lija answered.

Later in the week, the butler again met his master and brought up the subject of food. "Boss, I can tell you what vittles you gwine eat for dinner."

"Come to think of it," the master said, "the other day you predicted correctly what I was going to have for breakfast. Well, let us see if you can predict what I will have for dinner today."

Without hesitating, Lija said, "You gwine have fish and cornbread."

When the master was called to dinner, fish and cornbread were on the table. A few days after that the master met the owner of an adjoining plantation. "William," the master said, "I have a butler who I believe has a gift of prophesy."

"Oh, come now," William answered. "I'll bet you five hundred dollars you don't have a butler with such a gift."

"Yes, I really do believe Lija has the gift of prophesy," the master said. "I'll put up my five hundred dollars if you will put up yours."

"I'll do it," William said. "Give me your five hundred dollars and I will keep the money until I can test your butler."

After both men had put up their money, the master went home and told Lija what he had done. "I've got five hundred dollars on you and I don't want you to let me down. When William tests you, you had better tell him what he wants to know. And you had better be right."

Lija was worried. He couldn't bring himself to tell the master that he had looked in the kitchen and had seen what the cook was preparing for the meals. He couldn't confess that he had only been pretending to have prophetic powers. The master would surely punish him for that.

Every day Lija wondered if that would be the day he would be tested to see if he could foretell the future. He became sick with worry, so sick the master had a physician take a look at him. The doctor told the master Lija was not sick, and he didn't know why he was acting so strangely.

Finally the owner of the adjoining plantation sent for Lija to come to his plantation. Lija knew the day of reckoning had come. He tried frantically to think of some way to

get out of going, but he couldn't figure out a way to do so. Then it came to him to agree to go to the plantation, and perhaps, after he got there, he would think of a way to get out of the predicament.

While Lija was on the way to the plantation, William took a 'possum from a cage and put the wild animal under a tub. In order to test Lija and find out if he had psychic powers, William planned to ask Lija to identify the animal concealed under the tub. If the butler came up with the correct answer, Lija's master would win the bet. But if Lija couldn't say what kind of animal was under the tub, William would keep the money that had been put up by the planters.

"Well, Lija," William said when Lija arrived on his plantation, "let us see if you really do have the gift."

Lija wanted to run away, but he forced himself to listen to William.

"Now you see that tub over there." William indicated it with a nod. "When I lift the tub, what kind of animal will run out?"

Lija was in agony. He didn't know what kind of animal was under the tub. He wished he could die. He looked around, and then he looked toward the sky, and then he looked at the tub. It wasn't large enough to cover a dog. Besides, if a dog were under the container, the animal would be whining and nudging the vessel in an effort to escape. Just then Lija heard a bark come from a pen near the barn. So! William had put his hunting dogs in a pen. That could be to prevent them from barking and trying to get to the animal under the tub. But what kind of animal would the dogs most like to get to, Lija wondered. He knew that William, like most other planters, trained his dogs to run after 'coons and 'possums. So the animal in question must be a 'coon or a 'possum. But which one?

'Possums were used more often in the training of dogs than 'coons. Lija made his decision. "I b'lieve," he said, "you got the old 'possum now."

William lifted the tub and there was a 'possum! Lija jumped up. He sang out, "See there, I can tell the future. I can even tell you when judgment day is gwine come."

William looked at Lija with fear in his eyes.

"Yes," Lija said, realizing he had the upper hand now. "I can tell you the day you gwine die."

"Stop. Stop," William cried. "Go home," he said, pushing the thousand dollars into Lija's hand.

When Lija gave the money to his master, he said, "I told the kind of animal that be under the tub, and I can tell you the day of judgment. I can even tell you the day you gwine die!"

"Enough!" the master shouted. "Don't you tell me anything."

Lija was so excited over his ability to foretell the future that he lost all of his constraint and sang, right in the presence of the master, "Gwine grease my heels with tallow and lard, and slip and slide 'cross the white folks' yard!"

From that day on, Lija got anything he wanted from the master. All he had to do was lift a finger and say, "I can tell you the day you gwine die."

THE GHOST WHO RANG THE GATEHOUSE BELL

Ole Dan Tucker was a funny old man,
He washed his face in a frying pan,
He combed his hair with a wagon wheel
And died with a toothache in his heel.

THE DAN TUCKER IMMORTALIZED IN THIS FOLK SONG was the second governor of the Bermudas, and it was from Bermuda that a Daniel Tucker came to Litchfield Plantation in the late 1700s. Descendants of that Daniel Tucker owned the plantation, three miles west of Pawleys Island, until 1904.

There was no more remarkable family in the South Carolina Low Country than the Tuckers. Each generation was borne along on prosperity, and the gifts of fortune were lavished on them from the cradle to the grave.

The mansion stood in a grove of gnarled oak trees at the end of a deeply shadowed avenue of moss-draped oaks when the Tuckers took ownership of the property in the eighteenth century. Dan Tucker was a politician, and his plantation became well known during his years of ownership. When he died in 1797, he left Litchfield to three sons: John Hyrne, Daniel, and George. John Hyrne became the sole owner of the property after the deaths of Daniel and George.

John Hyrne Tucker was born on July 19, 1780. As a young man he suffered smallpox and was left with a face scarred from the pits of the sores. His blue-veined nose was of enormous size. But Tucker's appearance in no way impaired his opportunities for success in business and marriage. He acquired a great fortune, and during his life he married four times. On his death in June, 1859, he left Litchfield Plantation to a son, Dr. Henry Massingberd Tucker. Henry had been born in 1831 to John's third wife. Henry studied medicine and graduated from the South Carolina College at Columbia in 1851. Some member of almost every planters' family practiced medicine. Planters' sons were urged to study "physic" as "you can then save yourself the expense of doctors' bills on your plantation, and in your family," according to the mistress of a local plantation. And, like Dr. Tucker, most of the young physicians had done their medical study at the South Carolina College at Columbia.

Dr. Henry Tucker married Annie Manigault (MANNY-go). The couple had several children. The Tuckers owned a home "on the bay" in Charleston, and they spent time there during the winters when the crops were in. They also went there during hot summer months when it was considered unsafe to remain close to the rice fields, which bred mosquitoes. (Although it was not safe for the white people to remain on the plantations during the hot days, the slaves were considered immune to the malaria fever derived from the bites of mosquitoes.) In Charleston, the Tuckers attended the St. Cecilia balls and the Jockey Club ball, the latter winding up the horse-racing season.

Dr. Tucker was an Episcopalian and believed that the most proper place from which to go to heaven was the Episcopal Church. Litchfield Plantation was located adjacent to the property of All Saints Episcopal Church, and when the parishioners built a new church at All Saints, Dr.

Tucker had the old church building dismantled and moved to his plantation down the road. Plantation services for slaves were held in that building, and any slave who failed to answer the roll call at services did not receive his weekly allotment of pork, sugar, molasses, and tobacco unless illness had prevented his attendance.

Along with other local planters, Dr. Tucker joined clubs established for purposes of companionship. One such club was the Pee Dee Club and another was the Hot and Hot Fish Club, an unlikely name since the club was organized as a means to give the planters a place to gather and discuss their crops and the latest news of politics.

Dr. Tucker enjoyed pure, physical exercise in the open air. He believed such exercise was essential to "the health." He also took delight in riding a horse over his vast properties. But the sport of hunting wild animals and other game seemed to give him more pleasure than almost anything else. With his keen eyes, he could shoot accurately, and he trained dogs to search out the game birds he killed. He owned so many guns that he gave them names, and he won so many tournaments at the Georgetown Rifle Club that he finally declined invitations to participate in the competition.

Along with all his sporting activities, social life, and the practice of medicine, Dr. Tucker bestowed upon his family abundant attention and consideration. No better illustration of this can be given than the way in which he entered his home after a late-night medical call. Dr. Tucker was often summoned from his bed to make a call to a sickbed in the community. When he arrived home in the middle of the night, he would tap the gatehouse bell with his riding crop, and after the gateman had opened the gate, Dr. Tucker would get off his horse and walk to the mansion. In order not to disturb his family, he would go to his room on the second floor by way of a small, circular stairway he had

had constructed in a portion of the mansion that was away from the other bedrooms.

When the Civil War came, Dr. Tucker, like other Low Country planters, volunteered his services. He served as an officer and a gallant soldier throughout the four years of that war. He surrendered with Lee at Appomattox.

After the war, Dr. Tucker faced the problems of Reconstruction, but during this time he attended to the medical needs of the community as before. When he arrived home in the middle of the night, he tapped the gatehouse bell with his riding crop, then made his way to the mansion, going to his room on the second floor by way of the circular stairway.

Dr. Henry Massingberd Tucker died on January 10, 1904, and was laid to rest in the cemetery at Prince George Winyah Episcopal Church in Georgetown. At about the time of the death of Dr. Tucker, the days of fortunes based on rice culture were coming to an end.

One night shortly after Dr. Tucker's death, something mysterious happened. During the night, when the rain had been of long duration and moisture had gathered on the oaks and seeped down into the Spanish moss and dripped to the lane under the trees, the bell at the gate suddenly rang as though it has been tapped by a riding crop. The sound of the bell echoed in the avenue under the giant trees near the mansion. The people who lived nearby, half asleep, thought that Dr. Tucker had returned to Litchfield from a call to a sickbed.

That eerie incident was repeated each night thereafter. Some said that the ghost of Dr. Tucker had returned to Litchfield. Others claimed that the wind, the moisture, or the chill of the night was responsible for the ringing. Whatever the cause, there were many who waited in dread for that one chime each night. When the bell rang, for a moment all their fears rushed forward. But then, since

they knew the ringing was over for the night, their heart-beats slowed and their mouths were not so dry. They could settle down, knowing they wouldn't hear from the invisible caller for another twenty-four hours.

But the gatehouse bell rings no more. Litchfield Plantation is now a private residential development complete with villas, condominiums, private homes, a pool, a stable, and a marina on a Waccamaw River inlet. The manor house sits magnificently as it did in Dr. Tucker's day. Black wrought-iron gates by a brick gatehouse guard the entranceway. But the people around Litchfield Plantation can rest each night undisturbed, no longer tormented by that one, spine-tingling chime. The bell has been dismantled and taken away.

THE BLOODSTAINED BARN

A S I WRITE THIS, MY ONLY QUESTION ABOUT IT IS, LET me see now, can I remember it all? Listen to me. I was born in 1850. Great God! I write it now, what I saw with my own eyes.

Bloodstains!

Bloodstains of the dead. God knows, picture that! I can see the stains now, on the barn floor.

Tread them down; walk them out; wear them out; cover them up. All in vain! Who can tread out or cover up the bloodstains of the dead! Stains covered the wood floor, then they rose up through the hay.

My father worked in rice at Brookgreen Plantation. For Josh Ward, the biggest rice planter in the region. My father didn't have money, but he did have the key to the rice barn. And rice in the barn meant money!

My father had a head on him, and he went into the woods and made a pestle outa a pine limb. I had to go to the woods in the night to help him. I held a torch for him to see by when he put rice in the mortar and pestled it to get the hulls off. The rice my father took to the woods came outa the barn.

Before daybreak my father took a sack of rice and toted it to the boat and went to Georgetown and sold it. With the money he made on the rice he bought provisions, things like sugar and coffee. And some of the money he got from selling the rice he spent on liquor.

The overseer, named Fraser, somehow got wise to what my father was doing and was on the lookout for him. One morning as my father came back from Georgetown to the

Brookgreen boat landing, Fraser was waiting for him.

My father stepped from the boat to the landing, and when he saw Fraser looking straight at him he was so filled with fear he made a misstep and fell into the Waccamaw River. Fraser pulled him out of the river and threw him down on the landing.

"I'm on to you," Fraser snapped. "You been taking rice from the barn and selling it in Georgetown. And you been buying liquor with the money. And from the looks of you, you been sampling some of that liquor!" My father expected a lashing with the leather strap Fraser kept in the barn, but instead, the overseer helped him up and sent him to his cabin in the quarters.

The next Saturday morning, when all of us slaves took our places in line at the smokehouse to receive our rations, my father was near the end of the line. Fraser handed out meat, rice, grits, and meal in amounts allotted to each family according to the number of people in the family. When my father stepped up to get his share of the rations, Fraser went to a corner of the smokehouse and came back with a broken whiskey bottle. My father held out his hand for his rations, but the overseer pushed the jagged glass bottle into his hand. "That's your share of the rations this week," he said. My father was too scared to say anything back to him.

One day my mama saw the overseer and he gave her a task that was impossible for her to perform. She told him it would take two men to carry out the task. "Then meet me at the barn," the overseer snarled. "Be there at last light."

When my mama went to the barn, my father and I went with her. The overseer grabbed her by an arm and pushed her into a horse stall. "That's the bull pen," he growled. "Get in there!" He took a cowhide strap from the wall and popped it in the air. He barked at my mama, telling her to lie down so that her stomach rested on a block of wood. When she did that, he tied her hands and feet to pegs of wood he had hammered into the wood floor. "Now," the overseer said, "I'm going to give you a ride on the pony. You know that block of wood is a pony, don't you?"

I screamed out for Fraser to let my mama go, but the lash went up in the air, then came down on her back. Blood stained her dress.

Me and my father begged Fraser to stop lashing my mama, but he only laughed at us. "This is the bull pen," he said. "When someone is in the bull pen, they have to take a ride on the pony."

The overseer gave my mama forty lashes with the strap before he untied her hands and feet and let us take her home. As we left, I looked back. A pool of my mama's blood was on the barn floor.

Word spread round about of what the overseer had done to my mama, and the people in the quarters called for a meeting. They met in a cabin and called the meeting a "prayer meeting," but after a hymn and a prayer, they whispered about the brutish treatment of the overseer. Someone from almost every cabin had been a victim of his wrath. What could they do about him? That's what they tried to figure out. One thing for sure, they couldn't tell the master and missus about it because they were summering it on the French Broad River in the mountains of North Carolina. No one knew how long they would be gone. And the people from the quarters didn't know how much longer they could take the cruel treatment of the overseer. Someone said that freedom was coming, but that was probably just talk.

Some weeks passed, and the anger and the whispering slowly died down. Finally, the master and missus came back to the plantation from the French Broad River. Master Josh and Miss Bess were in good spirits, always laughing and talking and riding their horses. There was some talk in the quarters of getting someone to go to them and tell them about the overseer and the bloodstains on the barn floor. Since house servants enjoyed more prestige than field hands, one was asked to talk to them. But the servant was afraid. We never could persuade anyone to go to the master and missus about Fraser.

Christmastime came, and then there was some talk that the Yankees were coming. The master and missus left on the *Pilot Boy*, a rear-wheeler, and went to Marlborough County to wait for 'mancipation. With the owners gone, Fraser was again free to unleash his terror. My mama and father were taken to the bull pen. Fraser never failed to draw blood, and the blood spotted the barn floor.

Then one day the sound of a cannon roaring on the Waccamaw River shook the plantation, and the people in the quarters ran from their cabins. My father screamed for the people to have no fear. "Freedom's coming," he said. "You no longer will have the chains of slavery round your necks."

From all directions the people ran to the boat landing. They came from the quarters, from the manor house, from the rice fields, from the nurse house, where the babies were, and from the sick house.

A long, white boat stopped at the pier. As the people watched, a man stepped to the landing. The people said nothing, waiting to hear what the man had to say.

"This vessel is a Union ship, the *Catalpa*," he said. "I am the commanding officer."

Everyone was as still as an osprey sitting on her nest in the top of a Waccamaw cypress tree.

"Where is your master?" the officer asked.

"He went to Marlborough County," my father said.

"When do you expect him back?"

The people on the dock shook their heads. They did not know.

The officer lowered his voice. "You are free," he said. "Slavery has been abolished."

The people on the dock screamed, cried, shouted, and some of them prayed. A man threw a hat into the air, and it fell into the river. The officer held up a hand indicating for the people to be quiet and listen to him. "But freedom does not mean freedom from work. Go on with your work in the rice fields until your master returns. You can decide then whether to remain on the plantation or to leave. But I strongly advise you to wait until you have an opportunity to hear what your master has to say to you."

As soon as that Yankee boat left the dock, we went to the barn. We went to find Fraser. Oh my merciful God, we were treated so brutish all those years. Oh my Lord, he cut them so hard he just slashed their flesh right off. Now that freedom had come, we knew we had to get rid of the overseer.

But Fraser was not at the barn. The bloodstains were on the floor, but he was not there.

We went to the woods. If we found Fraser, we were going to put him across a log and beat him to death. We stayed until sunset, but we did not find Fraser. Fraser had run away to save his hide. We never saw him again.

We didn't want to pass through the barn. Bloodstains on the floor were remindful of the overseer. We tried to get rid of them. Tried to wash them off. Wash! Scrub! Stains came back. We walked back and forth. To and fro. Stomp! Stomp! Stains came back.

We covered the stains up with hay. Put hay all round and over them. Then there were bloodstains on the hay.

We wondered for Christ's sake why the bloodstains didn't leave. We tried everything. But years passed and still the blood remained.

It remained until 1930, when Archer Huntington came and bought Brookgreen Plantation and made Brookgreen Gardens. He saw the bloodstains and he tore down the barn. Yep. That was the first thing Huntington did when he bought the plantation. He tore down the barn. Until he did that, the bloodstains stayed right there.

About the Author

NANCY RHYNE is a native of Mount Holly, North Carolina. She divides her time between the two Carolinas, collecting stories, researching articles and enjoying the serenity of her Myrtle Beach home. She has visited the coasts of North and South America, Mexico, England and Greece and has found none more fascinating than the South Carolina coast. She has written articles and done research for dozens of publications, including *The New York Times, Town & Country* and *The Charlotte Observer.* Rhyne is currently a contributing editor for *Coast* magazine, and she is working on a book about South Carolina coastal plantations.